U0033925

新制多益閱讀搶分訓練營

3 STEPS 打造高效閱讀腦

解題技巧練習本

新制多益

閱讀搶分訓練營

3 STEPS 打造高效閱讀腦 解題技巧練習本 + 中譯解析本

作者 Park Hye-young / Jeon Ji-won / Joseph Bazil Manietta
譯者 劉嘉珮／關亭薇／蘇裕承
編輯 張盛傑
校對 吳思薇／陳慧莉
主編 丁宥暄
內頁排版 蔡怡柔
封面設計 林書玉
製程管理 洪巧玲
發行人 黃朝萍
出版者 寂天文化事業股份有限公司
電話 +886-(0)2-2365-9739
傳真 +886-(0)2-2365-9835
網址 www.icosmos.com.tw
讀者服務 onlineservice@icosmos.com.tw
出版日期 2024 年 4 月初版再刷 (0104)

토익 부스터 RC
Copyright © 2019 by Park Hye-young & Jeon Ji-won & Joseph Bazil Manietta
All rights reserved.
Traditional Chinese translation copyright © 2020 by Cosmos Culture Ltd.
This Traditional Chinese edition was published by arrangement with Darakwon, Inc.
through Agency Liang
版權所有　請勿翻印
郵撥帳號 1998620-0 寂天文化事業股份有限公司
訂書金額未滿 1000 元，請外加運費 100 元。
〔若有破損，請寄回更換，謝謝。〕

新制多益閱讀搶分訓練營：3 STEPS 打造高效閱讀腦 /
Park Hye-young, Jeon Ji-won, Joseph Bazil Manietta 著；
劉嘉珮，關亭薇，蘇裕承譯 . -- 初版 . -- [臺北市]：
寂天文化，2020.07
面；　公分
ISBN 978-986-318-921-3(平裝)

1. 多益測驗

805.1895　　109007817

作者序

「新制多益要怎麼準備才好呢？」

多益測驗改制後，我們最常從學生口中聽到的話，就是「多益突然變得好難」。同時，我們也看到不少學生讀完基礎教材後，在準備練習坊間出版的多益模擬題庫之時，就因為龐大的內容頓時頭昏眼花，甚至就此放棄。有鑑於此情況，我們為已經打下多益基礎，卻仍舊對準備多益測驗無所適從的學生們編寫了這本書。只要讀完本書，原本令你感到茫然的多益測驗，將能變得得心應手。

本書的特色如下：

- 以文法類別細分 14 個單元，每個文法類別下各彙整出 3 個必考的文法主題，每一主題均由**題型觀摩**切入講解相關文法，使讀者更容易理解。同時藉由基本**文法練習**、實際**試題演練**，幫助學習者確切掌握文法重點。
- 3 個文法主題介紹完後，都有一個**多益實戰詞彙**的單元，按照詞性依序介紹多益測驗高頻率詞彙。
- 每個章節最後收錄與多益試題形式相同的 PARTS 5、6、7 **實戰演練**題目，讀者可一邊複習該章節學到的文法、詞彙，一邊熟悉實際測驗模式。
- 最後附上一回 50 題的 **Half Test**，讓學習者在學完本書所有內容後，能夠透過模擬測驗來檢測自己的實力進步多少。

Park, Hye-young
Jeon, Ji-won

本書特色

STEP 1 題型觀摩

觀察實際題型，並研究**命題重點**，掌握該文法主題的初步概念。下面針對必備的基礎文法概念逐一解說，同時附上例句，幫助讀者熟悉重要的相關用法。

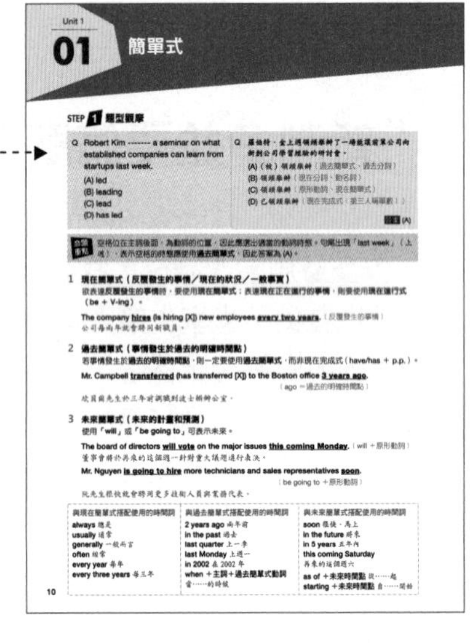

Unit 1
01 簡單式

STEP 1 題型觀摩

Q Robert Kim ------- a seminar on what established companies can learn from startups last week.
(A) led
(B) leading
(C) lead
(D) has led

Q 羅伯特・金上週領頭舉辦了一場能讓前輩公司向新創公司學習經驗的研討會。
(A)（被）領頭舉辦（過去簡單式、過去分詞）
(B) 領頭舉辦（現在分詞、動名詞）
(C) 領頭舉辦（原形動詞、現在簡單式）
(D) 已領頭舉辦（現在完成式：第三人稱單數）

答案 (A)

命題重點 空格位在主詞後面，為動詞的位置，因此應選出適當的動詞時態。句尾出現「last week」（上週），表示空格的時態應使用**過去簡單式**，因此答案為 (A)。

1 **現在簡單式（反覆發生的事情／現在的狀況／一般事實）**
欲表達反覆發生的事情時，要使用現在簡單式；表達現在正在進行的事情，則要使用現在進行式（be + V-ing）。
The company **hires** (is hiring [X]) new employees **every two years**.（反覆發生的事情）
公司每兩年就會聘用新職員。

2 **過去簡單式（事情發生於過去的明確時間點）**
若事情發生於**過去的明確時間點**，則一定要使用**過去簡單式**，而非現在完成式（have/has + p.p.）。
Mr. Campbell **transferred** (has transferred [X]) to the Boston office **3 years ago**.（ago＝過去的明確時間點）
坎貝爾先生於三年前調職到波士頓辦公室。

3 **未來簡單式（未來的計畫和預測）**
使用「will」或「be going to」可表示未來。
The board of directors **will vote** on the major issues **this coming Monday**.（will＋原形動詞）
董事會將於再來的這個週一針對重大議題進行表決。
Mr. Nguyen **is going to hire** more technicians and sales representatives **soon**.（be going to＋原形動詞）
阮先生很快就會聘用更多技術人員與業務代表。

與現在簡單式搭配使用的時間詞	與過去簡單式搭配使用的時間詞	與未來簡單式搭配使用的時間詞
always 總是 usually 通常 generally 一般而言 often 經常 every year 每年 every three years 每三年	2 years ago 兩年前 in the past 過去 last quarter 上一季 last Monday 上週一 in 2002 在 2002 年 when＋主詞＋過去簡單式動詞 當……的時候	soon 很快，馬上 in the future 將來 in 5 years 五年內 this coming Saturday 再來的這個週六 as of＋未來時間點 從……起 starting＋未來時間點 自……開始

10

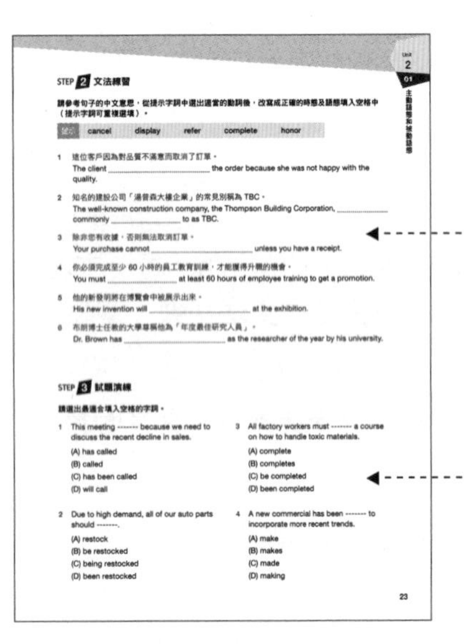

STEP 2 文法練習

請參考句子的中文意思，從提示字詞中選出適當的動詞後，改寫成正確的時態及語態填入空格中（提示字詞可重複選填）。

提示 cancel display refer complete honor

1 這位客戶因為對品質不滿意而取消了訂單。
The client __________ the order because she was not happy with the quality.

2 知名的建設公司「湯普森大樓企業」的常見別稱為 TBC。
The well-known construction company, the Thompson Building Corporation, __________ commonly __________ to as TBC.

3 除非您有收據，否則無法取消訂單。
Your purchase cannot __________ unless you have a receipt.

4 你必須完成至少 60 小時的員工教育訓練，才能獲得升職的機會。
You must __________ at least 60 hours of employee training to get a promotion.

5 他的新發明將在博覽會中被展示出來。
His new invention will __________ at the exhibition.

6 布朗博士任教的大學尊稱他為「年度最佳研究人員」。
Dr. Brown has __________ as the researcher of the year by his university.

STEP 3 試題演練

請選出最適合填入空格的字詞。

1 This meeting ------- because we need to discuss the recent decline in sales.
(A) has called
(B) called
(C) has been called
(D) will call

2 Due to high demand, all of our auto parts should -------.
(A) restock
(B) be restocked
(C) being restocked
(D) been restocked

3 All factory workers must ------- a course on how to handle toxic materials.
(A) complete
(B) completes
(C) be completed
(D) been completed

4 A new commercial has been ------- to incorporate more recent trends.
(A) make
(B) makes
(C) made
(D) making

Unit 2 01 主動語態和被動語態

23

STEP 2 文法練習

練習 3 到 6 題基本填空題／合併句子題，複習並鞏固剛剛在 STEP 1 學到的文法概念。

STEP 3 試題演練

演練 4 題與多益 **PART 5** 文法考題相同形式的單選題，掌握該文法概念在多益測驗中的出題方式。

多益實戰詞彙

PARTS 5、6 當中，除了有文法題之外也有詞彙題。因此，3 個文法主題介紹完後，都有一個以詞性分類的**高頻率詞彙**單元，讀者可背單字、做 10 題**選詞小練習**，輕鬆掌握多益必備詞彙。

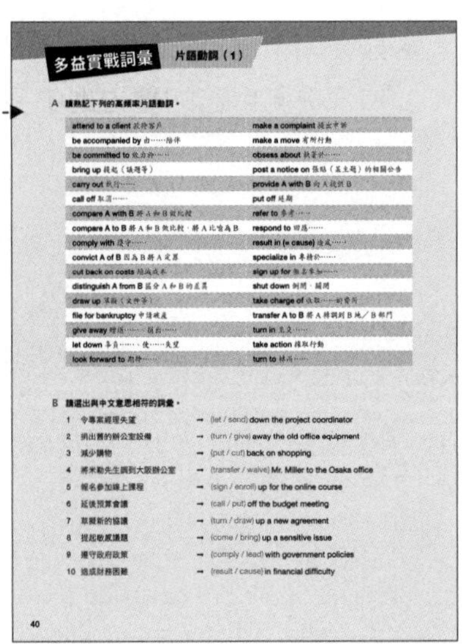

多益實戰詞彙 片語動詞（1）

A 請熟記下列的高頻率片語動詞。

attend to a client 接待客戶	make a complaint 提出申訴
be accompanied by 由……陪伴	make a move 有所行動
be committed to 致力於……	obsess about 執著於……
bring up 提起（議題等）	post a notice on 張貼（某主題）的相關公告
carry out 執行……	provide A with B 向 A 提供 B
call off 取消……	put off 延期
compare A with B 將 A 和 B 做比較	refer to 參考……
compare A to B 將 A 和 B 做比較，將 A 比喻為 B	respond to 回應……
comply with 遵守……	result in (= cause) 造成……
convict A of B 因為 B 將 A 定罪	specialize in 專精於……
cut back on costs 縮減成本	sign up for 報名參加……
distinguish A from B 區分 A 和 B 的差異	shut down 倒閉，關閉
draw up 草擬（文件等）	take charge of 負責……
file for bankruptcy 申請破產	transfer A to B 將 A 轉調到 B 地／B 部門
give away 贈送……，捐出……	turn in 呈交……
let down 辜負……，使……失望	take action 採取行動
look forward to 期待……	turn to 轉向……

B 請選出與中文意思相符的詞彙。

1 令專案經理失望 → (let / send) down the project coordinator
2 捐出舊的辦公室設備 → (turn / give) away the old office equipment
3 減少購物 → (put / cut) back on shopping
4 將米勒先生調到大阪辦公室 → (transfer / waive) Mr. Miller to the Osaka office
5 報名參加線上課程 → (sign / enroll) up for the online course
6 延後預算會議 → (call / put) off the budget meeting
7 草擬新的協議 → (turn / draw) up a new agreement
8 提起敏感議題 → (come / bring) up a sensitive issue
9 遵守政府政策 → (comply / lead) with government policies
10 造成財務困難 → (result / cause) in financial difficulty

40

實戰演練

收錄多益閱讀測驗三個大題的實戰演練試題。其中，PART 5 和 PART 6 利用文法概念和詞彙來命題，PART 7 則提供不同主題的文章和相關試題，供讀者做大量練習，將這些知識內化進入腦中。

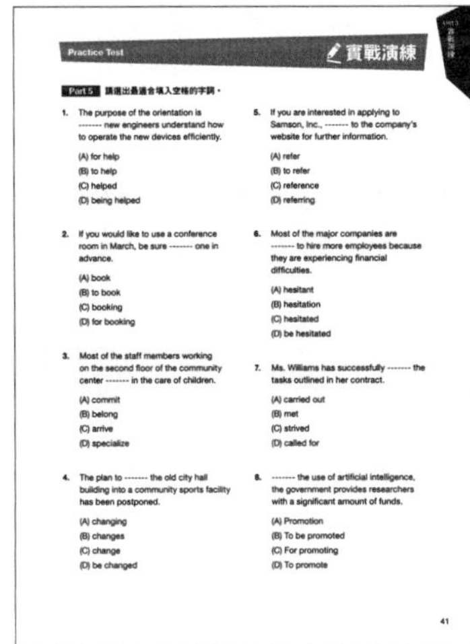

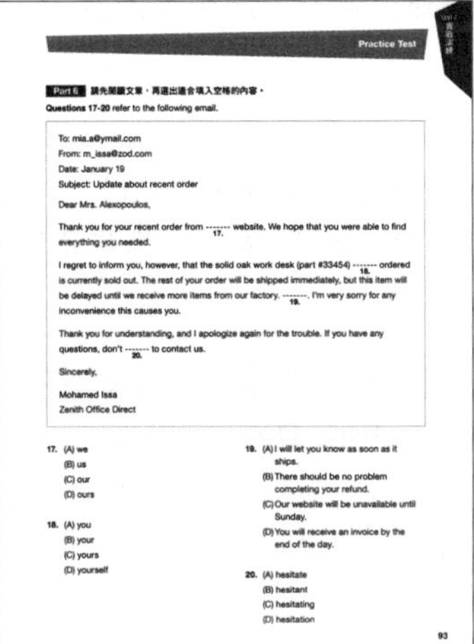

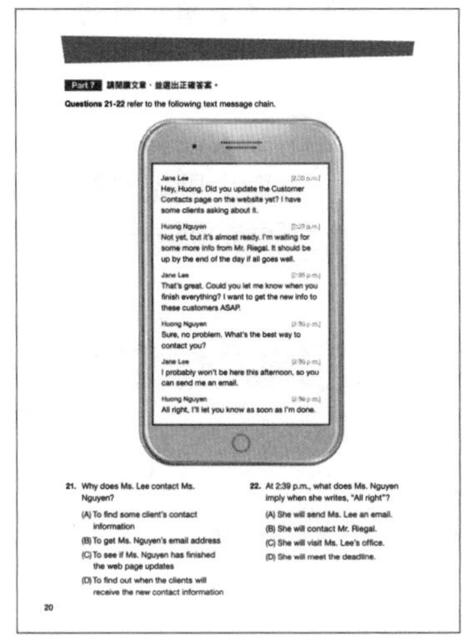

Half Test

學完本書的所有內容後，請做做看書末所附的 **50 題閱讀模擬測驗**，測試看看自己學到了多少。

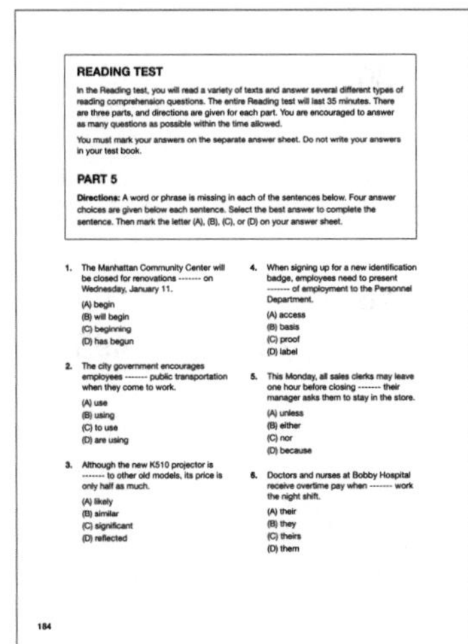

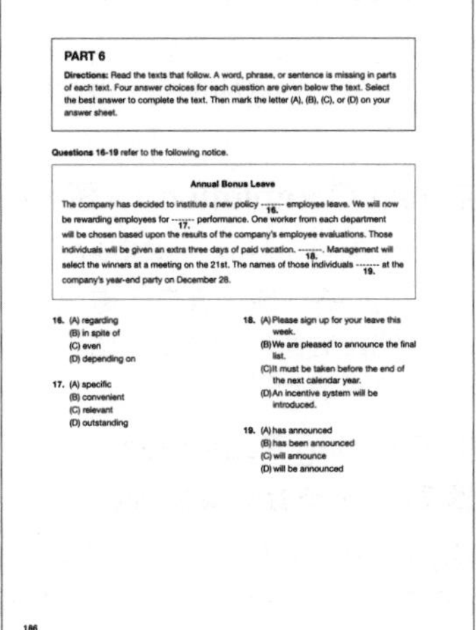

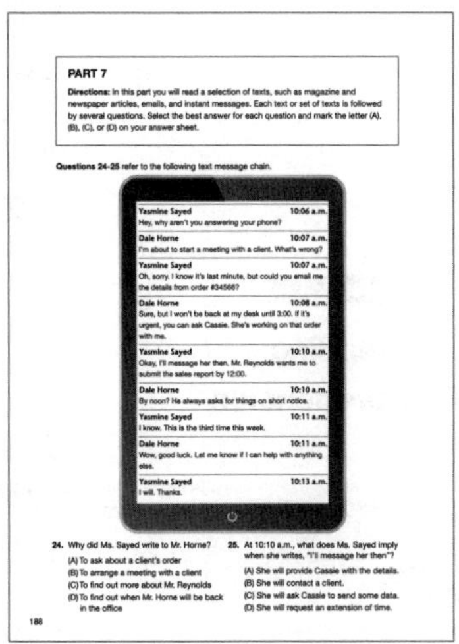

關於新制多益（NEW TOEIC）

新制多益是什麼呢？

TOEIC（多益）為 Test of English for International Communication（國際溝通英語測驗）的縮寫，針對英語非母語人士所設計，測驗其在國際環境中生活或執行工作時所具備的英語應用能力。2018 年 3 月起，改版的多益測驗——**NEW TOEIC（新制多益）**在台灣正式上路。測驗分數被廣泛作為人才招募、升遷、外派海外者等各項選拔之依據。

題型介紹

新制多益分為**聽力閱讀測驗（Listening & Reading Test）**及**口說寫作測驗（Speaking & Writing Test）**。**聽力閱讀測驗**為紙筆測驗，共 200 題單選題，測驗時間為 120 分鐘。聽力與閱讀兩者分開計時。

題型	PART	內容	題數	時間	分數
聽力測驗 Listening Comprehension	1	**照片描述 Picture Description** 一邊看試題冊上的照片，一邊聆聽錄音播放的四個選項，並從中選出最符合照片內容的選項。	6	45 分鐘	495 分
	2	**應答問題 Questions & Responses** 聆聽錄音播放的疑問句或直述句，以及對應的三個回答句或回應句，並從中選出最符合問答邏輯的選項。	25		
	3	**簡短對話 Short Conversations（3 題 X 13 組）** 聆聽兩人對話或三人對話，閱讀試題冊上的問題及四個答案選項（部分題組亦有圖表），並從中選出最符合問題的選項。	39		
	4	**簡短獨白 Short Talks（3 題 X 10 組）** 聆聽一段廣播、公告、演説或新聞報導，閱讀試題冊上的問題及四個答案選項（部分題組亦有圖表），並從中選出最符合問題的選項。	30		
閱讀測驗 Reading Comprehension	5	**單句填空 Incomplete Sentences** 閱讀一個英文句子，句中有一處空格，從四個選項中選出一個最符合空格的選項，以完成一個正確、完整的句子。	30	75 分鐘	495 分
	6	**短文填空 Text Completion（4 題 X 4 篇）** 閱讀一篇短文，內容可能是一篇電子郵件、一篇廣告或是一份説明書，當中會有四處空格（4 題），然後從每一題的四個選項中選出一個最適合填入空格的單字、片語或句子。	16		
	7	**閱讀測驗 Reading Passages（單篇閱讀 29 題＋多篇閱讀 25 題）** 單篇閱讀為一篇文章搭配 2 到 4 個問題，多篇文章則為兩篇或三篇有關聯性的文章搭配 5 個問題。文章內容可能是廣告、報紙上的報導、商業文件或公告。	54		
TOTAL			200	120 分鐘	990 分

命題方向

多益測驗考的是在日常生活和執行工作時所需的英語能力，因此考題也針對這兩大範圍出題。當中與商業有關的內容並不會涉及專業知識，同時也不會針對特定國家或文化出題。詳細的命題範圍如下：

一般商務（General Business）	簽約、協商、行銷、業務、企劃、會談
辦公場所（Office）	會議、信件、通知、電話、傳真、電子郵件、辦公室設備與用具
人事（Personnel）	求職、招聘、升遷、退休、支薪、獎金
財務（Finance and Budgeting）	投資、稅金、會計、銀行業務
生產（Manufacturing）	製造、工廠營運、品管
開發（Corporate Development）	研究調查、實驗、新品開發
採購（Purchasing）	購物、訂購、估價、結算
外食（Dining Out）	午餐、晚餐、聚餐、餐敘活動
健康（Health）	醫院、診斷、醫療保險
旅遊（Travel）	交通工具、住宿、車站與機場指南、預約與取消
娛樂（Entertainment）	電影、表演、音樂、美術、展覽
住宅／企業房產（Housing / Corporate Property）	建設、不動產買賣與租賃、電力與瓦斯相關服務

多益成績與英語能力對照

<table>
<tr><th>多益成績</th><th>英語能力</th><th>證書顏色</th></tr>
<tr><td>905-990 分</td><td>英文能力已十分近似英語母語人士，能夠流暢有條理地表達意見、參與對話、主持英文會議、調和衝突並做出結論，語言使用上即使有瑕疵，亦不會造成理解上的困擾。</td><td>金色（860-990）</td></tr>
<tr><td>785-900 分</td><td>可有效運用英語滿足社交及工作所需、措辭恰當、表達流暢；但在某些特定情形下，如面臨緊張壓力、討論話題過於冷僻艱澀時，仍會顯現出語言能力不足的狀況。</td><td>藍色（730-855）</td></tr>
<tr><td>605-780 分</td><td>可以用英語進行一般社交場合的談話，能夠應付例行性的業務需求，參加英文會議，聽取大部分要點；但無法流利的以英文發表意見、作辯論，使用的字彙、句型亦以一般常見者為主。</td><td rowspan="2">綠色（470-725）</td></tr>
<tr><td>405-600 分</td><td>英文文字溝通能力尚可、會話方面稍嫌詞彙不足、語句簡單，但已能掌握少量工作相關語言，可以從事英語相關程度較低的工作。</td></tr>
<tr><td>255-400 分</td><td>語言能力僅僅侷限在簡單的一般日常生活對話，同時無法做連續性交談，亦無法用英文工作。</td><td>棕色（220-465）</td></tr>
<tr><td>10-250 分</td><td>只能以背誦的句子進行問答而不能自行造句，尚無法將英語當作溝通工具來使用。</td><td>橘色（10-215）</td></tr>
</table>

目錄

Unit 1

動詞的時態

Tenses

01 簡單式

02 完成式

03 主詞動詞一致性的例外

★ 多益實戰詞彙：動詞 (1)

★ 實戰演練

01 簡單式

STEP 1 題型觀摩

Q Robert Kim ------- a seminar on what established companies can learn from startups last week.	Q 羅伯特·金上週領頭舉辦了一場能讓前輩公司向新創公司學習經驗的研討會。
(A) led	(A)（被）領頭舉辦（過去簡單式、過去分詞）
(B) leading	(B) 領頭舉辦（現在分詞、動名詞）
(C) lead	(C) 領頭舉辦（原形動詞、現在簡單式）
(D) has led	(D) 已領頭舉辦（現在完成式〔第三人稱單數〕）
	答案 (A)

空格位在主詞後面，為動詞的位置，因此應選出適當的動詞時態。句尾出現「last week」（上週），表示空格的時態應使用**過去簡單式**，因此答案為 (A)。

1 現在簡單式（反覆發生的事情／現在的狀況／一般事實）

欲表達**反覆發生的事情**時，要使用**現在簡單式**；表達**現在正在進行的事情**，則要使用**現在進行式**（be ＋ V-ing）。

The company **hires** (is hiring [X]) new employees **every two years**.〔反覆發生的事情〕
公司每兩年就會聘用新職員。

2 過去簡單式（事情發生於過去的明確時間點）

若事情發生於**過去的明確時間點**，則一定要使用**過去簡單式**，而非現在完成式（have/has ＋ p.p.）。

Mr. Campbell **transferred** (has transferred [X]) to the Boston office **3 years ago**.
〔ago ＝過去的明確時間點〕
坎貝爾先生於三年前調職到波士頓辦公室。

3 未來簡單式（未來的計畫和預測）

使用「will」或「be going to」可表示未來。

The board of directors **will vote** on the major issues **this coming Monday**.〔will ＋原形動詞〕
董事會將於再來的這個週一針對重大議題進行表決。

Mr. Nguyen **is going to hire** more technicians and sales representatives **soon**.
〔be going to ＋原形動詞〕
阮先生很快就會聘用更多技術人員與業務代表。

與現在簡單式搭配使用的時間詞	與過去簡單式搭配使用的時間詞	與未來簡單式搭配使用的時間詞
always 總是 usually 通常 generally 一般而言 often 經常 every year 每年 every three years 每三年	2 years ago 兩年前 in the past 過去 last quarter 上一季 last Monday 上週一 in 2002 在 2002 年 when ＋主詞＋過去簡單式動詞 當……的時候	soon 很快、馬上 in the future 將來 in 5 years 五年內 this coming Saturday 再來的這個週六 as of ＋未來時間點 從……起 starting ＋未來時間點 自……開始

STEP 2 文法練習

請參考句子的中文意思，從提示字詞中選出適當的動詞後，改寫成正確的時態填入空格中。

提示	work	receive	give	get	research	leave

1 週末上班的人會領到加班費。
Those who work on the weekend ________________ additional pay.

2 賈西亞先生演講結束後，將會給大家充裕的時間問問題。
Mr. Garcia ________________ plenty of time for questions after his speech.

3 「友紀電子公司」將於明年 1 月開始進行人工智慧科技的研究。
Yuki Electronics ________________ AI technology starting next January.

4 全體員工上週五都因一筆龐大訂單而加班。
Last Friday, all employees ________________ overtime because of a large order.

5 艾絲娜女士每天 7 點出門，8 點抵達公司。
Ms. Eisner ________________ home at 7 o'clock and ________________ to work at 8 o'clock every day.

STEP 3 試題演練

請選出最適合填入空格的字詞。

1 The Stratford Tourist Center ------- ferry rides along the Swan Canal twice a day.

(A) offer
(B) offers
(C) offering
(D) have offered

2 FM Industries ------- a reception to introduce the newly appointed sales manager to its employees last week.

(A) hold
(B) holds
(C) held
(D) has held

3 Venus Clothing, Inc. ------- its financial service provider as of March 1.

(A) change
(B) changing
(C) will change
(D) had changed

4 Brock's Dining ------- for a head chef to develop Italian cuisine for this coming summer.

(A) is looked
(B) looking
(C) is looking
(D) are looked

02 完成式

STEP 1 題型觀摩

Q Research shows that tourism at Kent National Park ------- stable over the past 3 years. (A) remains (B) remaining (C) has remained (D) had remained	**Q** 研究顯示，肯特國家公園過去三年來的觀光景氣已經維持穩定。 (A) 維持（現在簡單式〔第三人稱單數〕） (B) 維持（現在分詞、動名詞） (C) 已維持（現在完成式〔第三人稱單數〕） (D) 早已維持（過去完成式） 答案 (C)

題目空格為 that 子句中動詞的位置，而副詞片語「over the past 3 years」過去三年來表示「從過去到現在為止的一段時間」，要搭配**現在完成式**一起使用，因此答案為 (C)。

1 現在完成式

過去發生的事情持續到現在，或是**與現在有所關聯**時，須使用現在完成式。現在完成式表示**經驗、完成或持續**的概念。

與現在完成式搭配使用的副詞片語		
already 已經	so far 至今、到目前為止	for/over the past 5 years 過去五年來
just 剛才	until now 直到現在	not . . . yet 還沒有……
recently/lately 最近		

Mr. Vieira **has been** to Berlin more than 10 times **so far**.〔經驗：從過去到現在為止的經驗〕
維埃拉先生至今已經去過柏林十次以上。

The company **has developed** a system that can identify undervalued stocks.
〔完成：將過去開始做的事情完成〕
公司已經開發出一套系統，能夠有效確認被市場低估的股票。

Ms. Kwon **has served** as chief financial officer **for the last two years**.
〔持續：過去開始做的事情持續做到現在〕
權女士已經擔任財務長兩年了。

2 過去完成式

要表達**事情比過去所發生的某件事情更早發生**，須使用過去完成式。過去完成式常常搭配「**by the time ＋過去簡單式**」一起使用。

We **learned** that the company **had laid off** two of our colleagues.
我們聽說公司已經資遣了我們兩名同仁。

By the time Ms. Nichols **arrived** at the station, the train **had already left**.
妮可絲女士抵達車站時，火車早就已經開走了。

3 未來完成式

要表達**事情在未來某個特定時間點之前完成**，須使用未來完成式，常常搭配「**by the time ＋現在簡單式**」一起使用。

By the time Mr. Wilson **arrives**, all the participants **will have left** the conference.
等到威爾森先生抵達會議現場那時，所有與會者都將已經離開了。

STEP 2 文法練習

請參考句子的中文意思，從提示字詞中選出適當的動詞後，改寫成正確的時態填入空格中。

提示	meet	win	complete	visit	leave

1 柯爾先生以前從未造訪過倫敦辦公室。
Mr. Cole ____________ never ____________ the London office before.

2 坎培恩先生已經打贏過三次市長選戰。
Mr. Campion ____________________ mayoral elections three times.

3 新進員工至今都還沒見過公司的董事長。
The newly hired employees ____________________ the company president so far.

4 羅伯特先生回到辦公室時，他的客戶早就已經離開了。
By the time Mr. Roberto came back to his office, his client ____________________.

5 到了今年底，公司就會把道路工程完成。
By the end of this year, the company ____________________ the road construction.

STEP 3 試題演練

請選出最適合填入空格的字詞。

1 Mr. Eisner's investments in stocks ------- pretty lucrative over the past two years.

(A) are
(B) will be
(C) to be
(D) have been

2 By the time Ms. Gates got to the conference, Mr. Woo ------- his presentation.

(A) will already finish
(B) have already finished
(C) had already finished
(D) have already been finished

3 Dr. Carter ------- at Gray National University Hospital for the last twenty years, and he will retire this coming Friday.

(A) has served
(B) had served
(C) will have served
(D) serves

4 Because he ------- his job, he was able to sign up for the study abroad program.

(A) to quit
(B) quits
(C) quitting
(D) had quit

03 主詞動詞一致性的例外

STEP 1 題型觀摩

Q The consulting firm suggested that the company ------- its business to China. (A) has expanded (B) expands (C) expand (D) expanded	**Q** 顧問公司建議該公司將業務拓展至中國。 (A) 已拓展（現在完成式〔第三人稱單數〕） (B) 拓展（現在簡單式〔第三人稱單數〕） (C) 拓展（原形動詞、現在簡單式） (D)（被）拓展（過去簡單式、過去分詞） 答案 (C)

本題屬於主詞動詞單複數一致的例外情形。主要子句的動詞為 suggest（建議），後面**從屬子句省略了助動詞 should**，因此動詞位置須使用**原形動詞**，故答案為 (C)。只有知道這個文法規則，才能順利選出答案。其他表示**主張**、**建議**、**要求**之意的動詞，也適用於這個規則。

1 以現在簡單式代替未來式

即使主要子句的時態為未來式，**表示時間、條件的副詞子句**中仍須使用**現在簡單式動詞**。

表示時間及條件的副詞子句			
when 當……的時候	while 當……的時候	after 在……之後	before 在……之前
until 直到……	unless 除非……	as soon as 一……就……	
if/providing/provided 如果……、假使……		by the time 到……的時候	

We **will deliver** the items you ordered as soon as they **are** (will be [X]) available.

〔表示時間的副詞子句〕

只要您訂購的商品一有貨，我們就馬上出貨。

If you **fill** (will fill [X]) out the survey, we **will send** you a gift card valued at $50.

〔表示條件的副詞子句〕

如果您填寫問卷，我們將寄送價值 50 美元的禮品卡給您。

2 表示主張／要求／建議／命令的動詞＋ that ＋主詞＋（should）＋原形動詞

表示主張／要求／建議／命令之意的動詞		
suggest 提議	recommend 建議	advise 建議
insist 堅持	order 命令	request/require/demand 要求

The HR manager **requested** that employees (should) **update** (updated [X]) their personnel records.

人資部經理要求員工均應更新自己的人事紀錄。

3 表義務的形容詞＋ that ＋主詞＋（should）＋原形動詞

表示義務概念的形容詞		
important 重要的	necessary 必要的	imperative 當務之急的
essential 必要的	vital 非常重要的	

It is **imperative** that a new restaurant employee (should) **read** (reads [X]) the food safety guidelines.

餐廳新進員工當務之急要做的，就是詳讀食品安全處理規範。

STEP 2 文法練習

請參考句子的中文意思，從提示字詞中選出適當的動詞後，改寫成正確的時態填入空格中。

提示	come	keep	refine	wear	permit

1 安娜會等到史蒂芬醫師回到診所為止。
Anna will wait until Dr. Steven ______________ back to the clinic.

2 顧客把收據正本保管好，是很重要的一件事。
It is important that customers ______________ their original receipts.

3 這份報告建議公司改善製造程序。
The report suggests that the company ______________ its manufacturing procedures.

4 如果時間允許，我會在簡報結束後讓大家發問。
If time ______________, I will take questions after my presentation.

5 主辦單位要求參加者隨時配戴名牌。
The organizer required that attendants ______________ a badge at all times.

STEP 3 試題演練

請選出最適合填入空格的字詞。

1 Bob Textiles Co. has requested that we ------- the quantity of our order by Friday.

(A) confirm
(B) confirming
(C) confirmed
(D) will confirm

2 When the renovations -------, the Shanghai office of Wong, Inc. will return to its company building.

(A) will be completed
(B) are completed
(C) complete
(D) completing

3 It is vital that every construction worker ------- safety gear at all times.

(A) wore
(B) wear
(C) wears
(D) are worn

4 If Mr. Yamamoto ------- immediately after the meeting, he will arrive in time for the conference in New York.

(A) leaving
(B) leaves
(C) to leave
(D) had quit

多益實戰詞彙 動詞（1）

A 請熟記下列的高頻率動詞。

implement 實施、執行	disrupt 干擾
conduct 執行	increase 增加、提高
reserve 保留	possess 擁有、具有
enhance 加強	discontinue 停止、中斷
launch 推出、上市	estimate 估計
extend 延長	retain 維持
accommodate 容納	inquire 詢問、打聽
reach 達到	guarantee 保證
promote 促銷、將（某人）升職	disclose 揭露、透露
announce 宣布、公告	observe 觀察
feature 以……為特色	utilize 運用
release 釋出	distribute 分配
renew 更新	affix 貼上、固定
expire 過期	modify 修改
consult 諮詢	endorse 贊助、支持
attend 參加	exceed 超過
develop 開發、發展	accomplish 完成

B 請選出與中文意思相符的詞彙。

1 實施新政策 → (implement / develop) a new policy

2 預約飯店房間 → (renovate / reserve) a hotel room

3 延長上班時間 → (exceed / extend) the working hours

4 促銷新系列服飾 → (promote / endorse) a new line of clothes

5 更新勞動契約 → (extend / renew) an employment contract

6 參加畢業典禮 → (observe / attend) a commencement

7 干擾生產程序 → (disrupt / hesitate) production

8 提高效率 → (launch / increase) efficiency

9 維持公司名稱 → (retain / persist) the name of a company

10 有事情要宣布 → have something to (announce / accommodate)

Practice Test 實戰演練

Part 5 請選出最適合填入空格的字詞。

1. If the city council ------- us to hold a festival in the park, Mr. Kim will immediately start organizing the event.

(A) allows
(B) will allow
(C) allowing
(D) to allow

2. Ellen Jones, the new CFO at KP Bank, ------- in finance at a bank in England for more than 20 years.

(A) work
(B) working
(C) to work
(D) has worked

3. The technical support team requested that every employee ------- their passwords on a regular basis.

(A) change
(B) changes
(C) is changing
(D) are changing

4. Recently, Tom Construction Ltd. ------- more than 1,000 construction workers to build a massive factory in Texas.

(A) hires
(B) has hired
(C) will have hired
(D) had hired

5. Claire Myers ------- a bike-sharing company in Sydney, Australia.

(A) run
(B) runs
(C) to run
(D) running

6. Pica Technology successfully ------- the first stage of its new expansion plan last month.

(A) completes
(B) completed
(C) will complete
(D) has completed

7. The vice president ------- that some of the talented managers be transferred to the overseas branches in Europe.

(A) mentioned
(B) suggested
(C) thought
(D) considered

8. Please ------- the labels on the package so that they can be delivered by express mail service.

(A) affix
(B) drape
(C) transport
(D) launch

9. The Blackwell Animation Studio ------- the first computer animated feature film, *Toy Fairy*, in 1995.

(A) developing
(B) developed
(C) had developed
(D) has developed

10. If the new advertising campaign results in increased sales, the company ------- its sales goals for the year.

(A) is meeting
(B) will meet
(C) has met
(D) has been met

11. The venue for the company banquet can ------- over a hundred guests.

(A) accomplish
(B) accumulate
(C) acknowledge
(D) accommodate

12. Before the participants in the workshop entered the room, they ------- the guestbook.

(A) will sign
(B) signing
(C) was signing
(D) had signed

13. The summit between the leaders of the two countries ------- in Singapore at the moment.

(A) progresses
(B) is progressing
(C) will progress
(D) has progressed

14. The Valley Tech Corporation ------- additional factories in Southeast Asia, including in Vietnam and Indonesia, next year.

(A) construct
(B) constructing
(C) has constructed
(D) will construct

15. Management has decided to ------- Mr. Freeman to regional manager in Seoul.

(A) promote
(B) feature
(C) indicate
(D) observe

16. It is very ------- that every participant complete the questionnaire in detail.

(A) respectful
(B) educational
(C) important
(D) useful

Part 6 請先閱讀文章，再選出適合填入空格的內容。

Questions 17-20 refer to the following email.

To: m.suzuki@ymail.com
From: grace_ortiz@toronto.gov
Date: January 19
Subject: Awards Ceremony for Community Involvement

Dear Mr. Suzuki,

I am pleased to inform you that you have been selected by the city of Toronto to receive an award in recognition of your contributions to our community. Your donations to the park system and your role as a community leader ------- **17.** our city a better place to live. We would like to invite you to the awards ceremony at the Montgomery Convention Hall ------- **18.** December 6. We will present you and six other members of the community with awards. The event ------- **19.** dinner, so please let us know if you can make it or not. Again, congratulations on this achievement. ------- **20.**.

Sincerely,

Grace Ortiz
Community Outreach Director
City of Toronto

17. (A) are made
(B) have made
(C) making
(D) be making

18. (A) at
(B) on
(C) in
(D) to

19. (A) include
(B) including
(C) included
(D) will include

20. (A) I look forward to hearing from you soon.
(B) I will repay you for your financial contributions.
(C) You can park anywhere near the venue.
(D) You will be the only recipient of the award.

Part 7 請閱讀文章，並選出正確答案。

Questions 21-22 refer to the following text message chain.

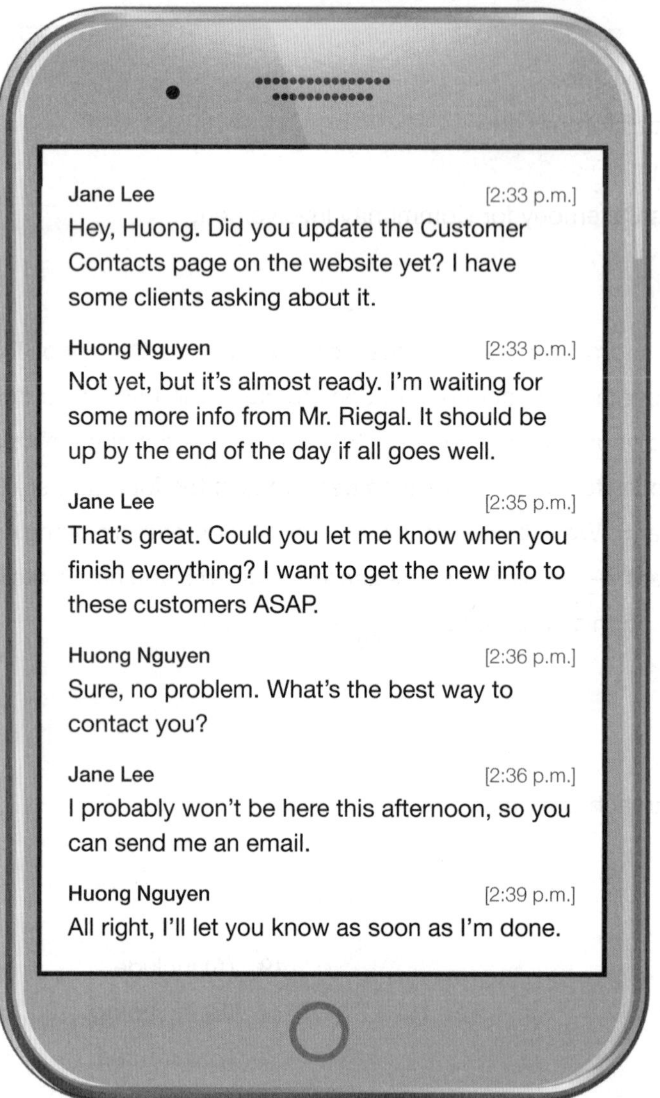

21. Why does Ms. Lee contact Ms. Nguyen?

(A) To find some client's contact information

(B) To get Ms. Nguyen's email address

(C) To see if Ms. Nguyen has finished the web page updates

(D) To find out when the clients will receive the new contact information

22. At 2:39 p.m., what does Ms. Nguyen imply when she writes, "All right"?

(A) She will send Ms. Lee an email.

(B) She will contact Mr. Riegal.

(C) She will visit Ms. Lee's office.

(D) She will meet the deadline.

Unit 2

主動語態和被動語態

Voices

01 主動語態和被動語態

02 授與動詞／不完全及物動詞的被動語態

03 須注意的被動語態用法

★ 多益實戰詞彙：動詞（2）

★ 實戰演練

Unit 2

01 主動語態和被動語態

STEP 1 題型觀摩

Q A sum of 500,000 dollars ------- to help those people who lost their homes due to the recent flood.

(A) donated
(B) to donate
(C) donates
(D) was donated

Q 各方捐贈總計達 50 萬美元來幫助最近因為水災而無家可歸的人。

(A)（被）捐贈（過去簡單式、過去分詞）
(B) 捐贈（不定詞 to V）
(C) 捐贈（現在簡單式〔第三人稱單數〕）
(D) 被捐贈（過去簡單式被動語態〔第一／三人稱單數〕）

答案 (D)

本題針對主動語態和被動語態的差異出題，**要先判斷主詞和動詞間的關係屬於主動還是被動，才能選出正確答案**。本題主詞「A sum of 500,000 dollars」（總計 50 萬美元的款項）為「被捐贈」的東西，因此答案為被動語態 (D)。(A) 可分析為過去分詞，但需要再補一個 be 動詞才能形成被動語態。

1 主動語態和被動語態的概念

(1) 主動語態：表示「主詞做了某行為」。

The organizer <u>prepared</u> a free meal for the participants at the seminar.〔主動語態的動詞〕
主辦單位為研討會的參與者準備了免費餐點。

(2) 被動語態：表示「對主詞做了某行為／主詞接受了某行為」，句型為「be 動詞＋過去分詞」。

The office <u>was renovated</u> for the first time in 30 years.〔被動語態的動詞〕
這間辦公室 30 年來第一次被整修。

2 被動語態的各類用法

種類	用法	例子
助動詞的被動語態	助動詞＋ be ＋過去分詞	can be seen 能被看見 will be made 將被進行
完成式的被動語態	have/has been ＋過去分詞	have been cleaned 已被清理 has been ignored 已被忽視
進行式的被動語態	am/is/are being ＋過去分詞	is being made 正在被進行 are being built 正在被修建

More efforts <u>will be made</u> to keep the environment safe.
大家將更努力維持環境安全。

The problem between the two parties <u>has been solved</u>.
雙方之間的問題已（被）解決。

Employee training <u>is being conducted</u> in Room 201.
員工教育訓練正在 201 號室（被）進行中。

STEP 2 文法練習

請參考句子的中文意思，從提示字詞中選出適當的動詞後，改寫成正確的時態及語態填入空格中（提示字詞可重複選填）。

提示	cancel	display	refer	complete	honor

1 這位客戶因為對品質不滿意而取消了訂單。
The client ______________ the order because she was not happy with the quality.

2 知名的建設公司「湯普森大樓企業」的常見別稱為 TBC。
The well-known construction company, the Thompson Building Corporation, ______________ commonly ______________ to as TBC.

3 除非您有收據，否則無法取消訂單。
Your purchase cannot ______________ unless you have a receipt.

4 你必須完成至少 60 小時的員工教育訓練，才能獲得升職的機會。
You must ______________ at least 60 hours of employee training to get a promotion.

5 他的新發明將在博覽會中被展示出來。
His new invention will ______________ at the exhibition.

6 布朗博士任教的大學尊稱他為「年度最佳研究人員」。
Dr. Brown has ______________ as the researcher of the year by his university.

STEP 3 試題演練

請選出最適合填入空格的字詞。

1 This meeting ------- because we need to discuss the recent decline in sales.

(A) has called
(B) called
(C) has been called
(D) will call

2 Due to high demand, all of our auto parts should -------.

(A) restock
(B) be restocked
(C) being restocked
(D) been restocked

3 All factory workers must ------- a course on how to handle toxic materials.

(A) complete
(B) completes
(C) be completed
(D) been completed

4 A new commercial has been ------- to incorporate more recent trends.

(A) make
(B) makes
(C) made
(D) making

02 授與動詞／不完全及物動詞的被動語態

STEP 1 題型觀摩

Q Every participant in the workshop ------- a free tote bag at the end. (A) gave (B) giving (C) was given (D) been given	**Q** 每位工作坊的學員下課時均拿到一個免費的托特包。 (A) 給予（過去簡單式） (B) 給予（現在分詞、動名詞） (C) 被給予（過去簡單式被動語態〔第一／三人稱單數〕） (D) 被給予（被動語態〔過去分詞形態〕） 答案 (C)

命題重點 主詞為 every participant（每位學員），而「tote bag」（托特包）為「被給出去」的東西，因此答案為被動語態 (C)。請注意，「被給予」＝「拿到」。授與動詞和不完全及物動詞的被動語態經常出現在考題中，請務必掌握其句型用法。

1 授與動詞的被動語態

授與動詞的句型為「主詞＋動詞＋間接受詞（通常是人／對象）＋直接受詞（通常是事物）」，由於該句型中有兩個受詞，其被動語態的句型亦有兩種表達方式。

具代表性的授與動詞			
give 給予	show 展示給……看	offer 主動提供	grant 授予
award 授予……獎項	lend 借出	pay 支付	

They **showed** me（間接受詞） a recently-renovated office（直接受詞）.

→ I **was shown** a recently-renovated office (by them).〔間接受詞變成主詞〕

→ The recently renovated office **was shown** to me (by them).〔直接受詞變成主詞〕

他們展示最近整修過的辦公室給我看。

2 不完全及物動詞的被動語態

不完全及物動詞的句型為「主詞＋動詞＋受詞＋受詞補語」。形容詞、名詞、不定詞等詞類皆可當作受詞補語，因此改寫成被動語態時，動詞的被動語態後面可以直接連接形容詞、名詞、不定詞等受詞補語。

不完全及物動詞的句型結構	主動語態→被動語態
主詞＋動詞＋受詞＋形容詞 例 keep 保持 consider 認為 make 使	Neighbors **consider** the new gym expensive. 鄰居們認為新開的健身房收費昂貴。 → The new gym **is considered** expensive by neighbors. 新開的健身房被鄰居們認為收費昂貴。
主詞＋動詞＋受詞＋名詞 例 name 命名 appoint 指派 elect 選出	They **appointed** him the floor manager. 他們指派他擔任樓管。 → He **was appointed** the floor manager. 他被指派為樓管。
主詞＋動詞＋受詞＋不定詞 to V 例 allow 允許 expect 預期、期待 force 強迫 remind 提醒 warn 警告 advise 建議 invite 邀請	They **expect** the president to come this Friday. 他們預期董事長本週五來訪。 → The president **is expected** to come this Friday. 董事長被預期本週五來訪。

STEP 2 文法練習

請參考範例，並按照提供的中文（均為主動語態）以及括號內的要求，改寫句子的主被動語態。

範例	他們示範新機器的使用方法給我看。 **They showed me how to use the new machine.** →（改成被動語態）**<u>I was shown how to use the new machine (by them).</u>**

1 他們頒予他比賽第二名的獎項。
They awarded him second place in the contest.
→（改成被動語態）...

2 他們將「羅伊餐廳」譽為鎮上最棒的中華餐廳。
Roy's Restaurant was named the best Chinese restaurant in town.
→（改成主動語態）...

3 董事會認為李女士適任新的管理職位。
The board of directors considers Ms. Lee suitable for the new management position.
→（改成被動語態）...

4 顧問團警告公司別再投入更多經費。
The company was warned not to invest more money by a group of consultants.
→（改成主動語態）...

5 他們允許俱樂部會員使用中心的零食吧，不須額外付費。
They allow club members to use the snack bar at the center at no extra charge.
→（改成被動語態）...

STEP 3 試題演練

請選出最適合填入空格的字詞。

1 Customers are ------- to use public transportation since there are not enough parking spaces.
(A) advising
(B) advisory
(C) advised
(D) advise

2 Ms. Flint was ------- the grand prize for her performance at the show.
(A) award
(B) awards
(C) awarding
(D) awarded

3 The new sign-in system is considered ------- by most of the employees.
(A) convenient
(B) convenience
(C) conveniently
(D) convinced

4 People working in the building are ------- to eat at the newly renovated cafeteria.
(A) encourage
(B) encouraging
(C) encouraged
(D) encouragement

03 須注意的被動語態用法

STEP 1 題型觀摩

Q The new conference room is equipped ------- a computer projector and a screen.

(A) with
(B) to
(C) of
(D) from

Q 新的會議室配備有一台電腦投影機和一個螢幕。

(A) with
(B) to
(C) of
(D) from

答案 (A)

命題重點 以被動語態句型命題的考題中，空格置於介系詞位置時，答案除了 by 之外，也有可能是其他的介系詞。本題的句型為被動語態，而值得留意的是「be equipped with」表示「配備有……」的意思，**介系詞要使用 with，而非 by**。

須注意的被動語態用法

be ＋過去分詞＋ with	be ＋過去分詞＋ in	be ＋過去分詞＋ to
be satisfied with 對……感到滿意 be covered with 覆蓋著…… be filled with 充滿著…… be pleased with 對……感到開心／滿意 be obsessed with 執著於…… be equipped with 配備有……	be interested in 對……感興趣 be involved in 涉入…… be engaged in 參與…… be absorbed in 埋首於…… be indulged in 沉迷於…… be skilled in 專精於……	be known to 為（某人）所知 be devoted to 致力於…… be committed to 致力於…… be exposed to 暴露於…… be accustomed to 適應…… be used to 習慣…… be related to 與……有關 ※以上的 to 皆為介系詞，後接名詞或動名詞。

If you **are** not **satisfied with** the service, you should call the customer service office.
如果你對服務感到不滿意，應聯絡客服部。

Some children **are absorbed in** playing new mobile games.
有些兒童埋首於新的手遊。

Dr. Jin **is devoted to** helping people who are in need of personal care.
珍醫師致力於協助需要個人照護的人。

STEP 2 文法練習

請參考句子的中文意思，從提示字詞中選出適當的片語後，改寫成正確的形態填入空格中。

提示			
	be devoted to	be filled with	be engaged in
	be involved in	be equipped with	be used to

1 這間工廠配備有最新的設施。
The factory ________________ up-to-date facilities.

2 博物館充滿著來自世界各地的遊客。
The museum ________________ tourists from all around the world.

3 有些人不習慣靠道路左邊行駛。
Some people ____________ not ________________ driving on the left side of the road.

4 我的合夥人參與了業務拓展事宜。
My partner ________________ the expansion of the business.

5 如果此醜聞牽涉到你，你必須向經理報告。
If you ________________ the scandal, you have to report it to the manager.

STEP 3 試題演練

請選出最適合填入空格的字詞。

1 Jack's Bistro is ------- to using the best-quality ingredients in all of its dishes.
(A) devote
(B) devotes
(C) devotion
(D) devoted

2 Research shows that some of the workers are ------- to a great deal of toxic gas near the assembly line.
(A) expose
(B) exposes
(C) exposed
(D) exposing

3 It turned out that our product is known only ------- those who live in urban areas.
(A) with
(B) at
(C) to
(D) for

4 If you are ------- in signing up for the workshop on the new software program, please talk to your supervisor.
(A) interest
(B) interests
(C) interesting
(D) interested

多益實戰詞彙 動詞（2）

A 不及物動詞後面不能直接連接受詞，若要連接受詞，得搭配介系詞一起使用。請熟記下列的「不及物動詞」和「不及物動詞＋介系詞」組合。

不及物動詞	不及物動詞＋介系詞
be 是…… become 成為	account for 說明……、占（某比例）
remain 維持	agree to 認同……
seem/appear 似乎	care for 照料……
go 出發 depart 離去	deal with 處理……、應對……
come 來到 arrive 抵達	depend on 依賴（某人）、依（某事）而定
happen 發生	participate in 參與……
occur / take place 發生	react to 對……反應
decrease/decline/fall 減少	specialize in 專精於……
increase/rise/grow 增加	belong to 屬於……
exist 存在	subscribe to 訂閱……、訂購……
do 做	object to 反對……
count 要緊	look over 查看……
work 奏效	apply to 應徵（公司）、適用於…… apply for 應徵（工作）、申請（獎學金等）

B 請選出與中文意思相符的詞彙。

1 應徵公司 → (apply to / agree to) the company

2 參與活動 → (care for / participate in) the event

3 反對提案 → (object to / look over) the proposal

4 專精於行銷 → (subscribe to / specialize in) marketing

5 增加預算 → (deal with / increase) the budget

6 說明理由 → (count / account for) the reason

7 藥物奏效 → the medicine (exists / works)

8 發生意外 → an accident (happens / remains)

9 依情況而定 → (depend on / belong to) the situation

10 處理問題 → (agree to / deal with) problems

Practice Test 實戰演練

Part 5 請選出最適合填入空格的字詞。

1. Mr. Smith was ------- as the employee of the year thanks to his dedication to the company.

   (A) honor
   (B) honoring
   (C) honored
   (D) honors

2. Action must be ------- with regard to a recent decrease in the number of customers.

   (A) take
   (B) taken
   (C) taking
   (D) took

3. Your subscription can be ------- at any time by submitting a request for cancelation by email or mail.

   (A) terminate
   (B) terminating
   (C) termination
   (D) terminated

4. It seems that no one objects ------- decreasing retail prices in our shop.

   (A) to
   (B) with
   (C) over
   (D) from

5. The manager usually ------- over the documents before she makes a decision.

   (A) looks
   (B) accounts
   (C) does
   (D) counts

6. The development of writing was ------- mostly by merchants and accountants.

   (A) pioneer
   (B) pioneering
   (C) pioneered
   (D) be pioneered

7. The problem will ------- with care because it is considered an extremely sensitive issue.

   (A) to deal
   (B) deal
   (C) be dealt
   (D) be dealing

8. The client was not pleased ------- the new bedsheets, so she requested that the length be shortened.

   (A) on
   (B) with
   (C) at
   (D) for

9. You should write your name and date to make sure you are ------- the projector.

(A) give

(B) gave

(C) given

(D) giving

10. The R&D team ------- to back up all the files so that they would not lose any important data.

(A) reminded

(B) was reminded

(C) will remind

(D) reminding

11. Before renovations take place, all the offices must ------- by Friday at the latest.

(A) vacate

(B) vacating

(C) vacancy

(D) be vacated

12. Employee morale is closely ------- to the office atmosphere where they work.

(A) relate

(B) relates

(C) related

(D) relating

13. If any accident ------- on a public road, the state assumes no liability.

(A) occurs

(B) accounts

(C) works

(D) reacts

14. It is not ------- to park in front of the building due to the remodeling process of the main entrance.

(A) permit

(B) permits

(C) permitted

(D) permission

15. The Owen & Silver Travel Agency is ------- to providing you with the best experience possible.

(A) dedicate

(B) dedicated

(C) dedicating

(D) dedication

16. We are truly delighted to share that we have ------- first prize at the 2019 Teaching Excellence Competition.

(A) been awarding

(B) been awarded

(C) was awarded

(D) been award

Part 6 請先閱讀文章，再選出適合填入空格的內容。

Questions 17-20 refer to the following email.

Dear residents:

We would like to inform you that the north parking lot -------(17.) for construction from March 12 to 17. This construction is part of the spring remodeling project, and the north lot is the first one to be renovated. During this time, we ask that all residents move their cars to the east or south parking lots. -------(18.). Any cars that are not -------(19.) to one of these three sites by March 12 at 9:00 a.m. will be towed to prevent delays in construction. Thank you, and we apologize for the -------(20.).

17. (A) will close
(B) will be closing
(C) will be closed
(D) are closed

18. (A) Construction will be paid for by the monthly residence fee.
(B) No guests will be permitted onsite during the construction period.
(C) You can expect the next construction project to begin early next week.
(D) Additionally, we will be providing extra parking space on Elm Street.

19. (A) move
(B) moves
(C) moved
(D) to be moving

20. (A) inconvenience
(B) appliance
(C) competition
(D) approval

Part 7 請閱讀文章，並選出正確答案。

Questions 21-23 refer to the following letter.

Omaha Municipal Museum of Natural History
555 German Hill Rd.
Omaha, Nebraska 55568
www.omahamuseums.com

Dear Mrs. Williams,

Thank you for your continued financial support of the museum. — [1] —. As thanks, we would like to invite you to our 15th annual Night at the Museum event. More than 200 museum donors will come together to enjoy an evening in the main exhibition hall that includes a cocktail reception, live music, a seated dinner, and an awards presentation. — [2] —.

This special event has limited space, so please RSVP by December 21 online at www.omahamuseums.com/RSVP or by phone at 084-857-2453. — [3] —. Also, please inform us if you will bring a guest or not. Attendees are allowed to bring one guest.

Thank you again for your continued support, and we look forward to hearing from you soon. — [4] —.

Sincerely,
Jacob Lutz
Omaha Municipal Museum of Natural History
Community Outreach Director

21. Why did Mr. Lutz write to Mrs. Williams?

(A) To offer her a discount at a future exhibition
(B) To ask for her food preferences
(C) To offer her a chance to attend to a museum-hosted event
(D) To ask her to donate regularly to the museum

22. What is suggested about Mrs. Williams?

(A) She will attend a special event at the museum.
(B) She has made a donation to the museum.
(C) She visits the museum very often.
(D) She will receive an award for helping the museum.

23. In which of the position marked [1], [2], [3], and [4] does the following sentence best belong?

"When replying, please let us know your meal preference."

(A) [1]
(B) [2]
(C) [3]
(D) [4]

Unit 3

不定詞 to V

to-infinitive

01 不定詞 to V 的用法

02 不定詞 to V 作為動詞的受詞／受詞補語

03 不定詞 to V 的慣用語

★ 多益實戰詞彙：片語動詞（1）

★ 實戰演練

01 不定詞 to V 的用法

STEP 1 題型觀摩

Q ------- the designs of the new products, the director will hold a meeting early next week.	Q 為了改善新產品的設計，總監將於下週初召開會議。
(A) To improve	(A) 為了改善（不定詞 to V）
(B) For improving	(B) 關於改善（介系詞 for ＋動名詞）
(C) To be improved	(C) 被改善（被動語態〔不定詞 to V 形態〕）
(D) Improve	(D) 改善（原形動詞、現在簡單式）
	答案 (A)

命題重點 不定詞考題類型中，出題頻率最高的類型為**不定詞 to V 的副詞用法**，用來表示**「目的」**。在此用法中，不定詞 to V 解釋為**「為了……」**，可放在句首、句尾或句中。根據題意，用主動語態表達「總監為了『改善』設計」較為適當，因此答案為 (A)。

1 名詞用法：扮演名詞的角色（當作主詞／受詞／補語）

不定詞為「to ＋原形動詞」。在名詞用法中，不定詞的功能與**名詞**相同，扮演**主詞**、**受詞或補語**的角色。

主詞	**<u>To renovate</u>** the old historical museum will be challenging. 整修老舊的歷史博物館，會是一大挑戰。
受詞	The finance team manager agreed **<u>to give</u>** Mr. Smith a pay raise. 財務團隊的經理決定幫史密斯先生加薪。
補語	The purpose of the training program is **<u>to provide</u>** employees with the latest technology. 這個訓練課程的目的在於讓員工熟悉最新科技。

2 形容詞用法：用來修飾名詞

不定詞扮演形容詞的角色時，可以放在名詞後面，用來**修飾名詞**。

經常搭配不定詞使用的名詞（名詞＋不定詞 to V）

work to V 要（做、完成等）的工作	chance to V 做……的機會	opportunity to V 做……的機會
decision to V 做……的決定	ability to V 做……的能力	plan to V 做……的計畫
right to V 做……的權利	way to V 做……的方法	attempt to V 做……所需要的嘗試

The decision **<u>to invest</u>** in foreign stock markets was made by the CEO.
執行長做出了投資海外股市的決定。

3 副詞用法：表示目的或原因

不定詞表示**「目的」**時，意思為**「為了……」**，可與**「in order to」**替換使用。若不定詞放在 pleased（開心的、滿意的）、glad（高興的）、delighted（愉快的）等表達情緒的形容詞後面時，則用來表示**引發該情緒的「原因」**。

<u>To promote (= In order to promote)</u> online sales, we are planning promotional events.〔目的〕
為了提高線上銷售量，我們正在規劃促銷活動。

The author was pleased **<u>to hear</u>** that her new book is selling well.〔原因〕
這位作家聽到自己的新著作大賣非常開心。

STEP 2 文法練習

請參考句子的中文意思，從提示字詞中選出適當的動詞後，改寫成正確的形態填入空格中。另外，請選出該句屬於哪一種不定詞的用法。

提示	recruit	increase	work	meet	receive

1 新進員工本週將有見到董事長的機會。
The newly hired employees will have a chance ________ the president this week.
（名詞用法 | 形容詞用法 | 副詞用法）

2 這家公司因為業績下滑，而無法負擔招聘高階主管的經費。
The company can't afford ________ high-level executives because of the decrease in sales.
（名詞用法 | 形容詞用法 | 副詞用法）

3 「KTEC 公司」將會努力提高顧客的滿意度。
KTEC Co. will make an effort ________ customer satisfaction.
（名詞用法 | 形容詞用法 | 副詞用法）

4 對於行銷人員而言，與同事和諧共事極其重要。
________ harmoniously with coworkers is extremely important for marketers.
（名詞用法 | 形容詞用法 | 副詞用法）

5 若想要退款，請務必出示有效收據。
________ a refund, a valid receipt must be presented.
（名詞用法 | 形容詞用法 | 副詞用法）

STEP 3 試題演練

請選出最適合填入空格的字詞。

1 Regular customer surveys are an excellent way ------- customers' needs.
(A) to understand
(B) understanding
(C) of understand
(D) has understood

2 Management has decided ------- a couple of new offices in European countries.
(A) opening
(B) to open
(C) has opened
(D) is opening

3 The manager will be meeting with the top candidates ------- a few more questions.
(A) asked
(B) to ask
(C) to asking
(D) for asking

4 The labor union was pleased ------- the offer of an 8% pay raise.
(A) accepts
(B) for accepting
(C) to accepting
(D) to accept

02 不定詞 to V 作為動詞的受詞／受詞補語

STEP 1 題型觀摩

Q A German carmaker failed ------- emissions of diesel fumes that can cause lung diseases. (A) reduce (B) reducing (C) to reduce (D) reduces	Q 某德國汽車工廠未能減少可能會導致肺病的柴油廢氣排放量。 (A) 減少（原形動詞、現在簡單式） (B) 減少（現在分詞、動名詞） (C) 減少（不定詞 to V） (D) 減少（現在簡單式〔第三人稱單數〕） 答案 (C)

命題重點 空格前面為動詞 fail（未能……），該動詞後面要**連接不定詞 to V**，不能連接動名詞，因此答案為 (C)。請熟記這類以不定詞作為受詞的動詞。

1 以不定詞作為受詞的動詞（動詞＋不定詞 to V）

hope to V 希望做（某事）	afford to V 負擔得起做（某事）
need to V 需要做（某事）	offer to V 主動提議做（某事）
want to V 想要做（某事）	expect to V 期待做（某事）
agree to V 同意做（某事）	manage to V 設法做（某事）
plan to V 計畫做（某事）	ask to V 請求做（某事）
decide to V 決定做（某事）	fail to V 未能做到（某事）
choose to V 選擇做（某事）	refuse to V 拒絕做（某事）

Everyone in the HR Department **agreed to hold** this year's employee awards banquet in March.
人資部的每位同仁均同意於 3 月舉辦今年的員工頒獎宴會。

2 以不定詞作為受詞補語的動詞（動詞＋受詞＋不定詞 to V）

ask ＋受詞＋ to V 請求（某人）做（某事）	expect ＋受詞＋ to V 期待（某人）做（某事）
tell ＋受詞＋ to V 叫（某人）做（某事）	enable ＋受詞＋ to V 使（某人）能夠做（某事）
remind ＋受詞＋ to V 提醒（某人）做（某事）	require ＋受詞＋ to V 要求（某人）做（某事）
advise ＋受詞＋ to V 建議（某人）做（某事）	allow ＋受詞＋ to V 允許（某人）做（某事）
invite ＋受詞＋ to V 邀請（某人）做（某事）	encourage ＋受詞＋ to V 鼓勵（某人）做（某事）
force ＋受詞＋ to V 強迫（某人）做（某事）	help ＋受詞＋ (to)* V 幫助（某人）做（某事）
	*help 後面的 to V，to 可省略。

The engineering team **advised employees to back up** all their files on a regular basis.
工程團隊建議員工定期備份所有檔案。

The secretary **reminded Mr. Takeshi to call** JK Bank at 3 o'clock.
秘書提醒武史先生於 3 點打電話給「JK銀行」。

STEP 2 文法練習

請參考句子的中文意思，從提示字詞中選出一組適當的動詞後，改寫成正確的動詞時態並加上不定詞，再填入空格中。

提示			
	remind / come	plan / interview	want / work
	ask / transfer	help / adjust	expect / set up

1 人事經理打算於再來這個週二面試數名應徵者。
The personnel manager is ________________ several candidates this coming Tuesday.

2 「WCK有限公司」期待我們能為新專案召開會議。
WCK Ltd. is ____________ us ________________ a meeting with regard to the new project.

3 泰勒女士已提出轉調至倫敦辦公室的請求。
Ms. Taylor has ________________ to the London office.

4 大多數的職員都想到海外工作，以精進自己的事業前景。
A majority of the staff members ________________ abroad to improve their career prospects.

5 導遊提醒我們中午前須回到車站。
The tour guide ____________ us ________________ back to the station by midday.

6 入職訓練課程能協助新進員工適應職場。
The induction course will ____________ new employees ________________ themselves to the workplace.

STEP 3 試題演練

請選出最適合填入空格的字詞。

1 KC Finance encourages its analysts ------- for the World Economic Forum.

(A) register
(B) to register
(C) registering
(D) to be registered

2 Realwork Solutions needs ------- at least two more programmers to meet the deadline.

(A) hire
(B) hiring
(C) to hire
(D) to have hired

3 Management expects Human Resources ------- several charity events this year.

(A) organizing
(B) to organize
(C) be organized
(D) to be organized

4 Some officials agreed ------- the funds to construct more community facilities.

(A) to spend
(B) to spending
(C) spending
(D) on spend

03 不定詞 to V 的慣用語

STEP 1 題型觀摩

Q The modern art exhibition is scheduled ------- place on July 2. (A) take (B) taking (C) to take (D) takes	**Q** 現代藝術展預定於 7 月 2 日舉行。 (A) 舉行（原形動詞、現在簡單式） (B) 舉行（現在分詞、動名詞） (C) 舉行（不定詞 to V） (D) 舉行（現在簡單式〔第三人稱單數〕） 答案 (C)

命題重點 多益測驗中，不定詞 to V 的慣用語經常會出現在考題中。本題中，只要知道「be scheduled to V」（預計做某事）的用法，便能輕鬆解題，因此請記下這類慣用語。

1 too ＋形容詞／副詞＋ to V（太……以致於不能……）

當題目要求選出適合放在「too . . . to V」之間的詞彙時，請依照題意判斷，並選出適當的副詞或形容詞。

The new accounting system is **too difficult to understand**. 〔too ＋形容詞〕
新的會計系統太過困難，完全無法理解。

The documents were written **too terribly** for us* **to read**. 〔too ＋副詞〕
因為文件內容寫得太糟了，所以我們看不懂。

*不定詞前面加上「for ＋受格」，表示不定詞意義上的主詞。

2 形容詞／副詞＋ enough to V（夠……足以……）

Most of my colleagues are **intelligent enough to do** the project. 〔形容詞＋ enough〕
我多數同仁的才智均足以勝任這項專案。

Mr. Jackson performed **well enough to get** a promotion. 〔副詞＋ enough〕
傑克森先生的表現極佳而足以獲得升職。

3 「be 動詞＋形容詞＋不定詞 to V」的慣用語

be able to V 有能力做（某事）	be eager to V 熱切做（某事）
be likely to V 很有可能做（某事）	be willing to V 願意做（某事）
be scheduled to V 預定做（某事）、安排好做（某事）	be eligible to V 有資格做（某事）
be about to V 將要做（某事）	be hesitant to V 猶豫要不要做（某事）
be supposed to V 應該做（某事）	be sure to V 一定要做（某事）
be ready to V 準備好要做（某事）	be apt to V 常做（某事）

18-year-olds **are** not **eligible to vote** in Taiwan.
台灣的 18 歲青年不具投票資格。

STEP 2 文法練習

請參考句子的中文意思，使用 too / enough / willing / about 加上提示字詞，並搭配不定詞一起填入空格中。

提示	costly	expensive	clearly	purchase	understand	accept	begin

1 波音的新機型太過昂貴，所以我們買不起。
The new airplane from Boeing is ------------------------ for us ------------------------
------------------------.

2 這位政府官員清楚說明了公告內容，方便閱聽人理解。
The official made an announcement ------------------------ for the audience ------------------------
------------------------.

3 將所有存貨儲放在倉庫的成本太高了。
It is ------------------------ to store all the inventory in the warehouses.

4 珍娜．尼克森願意接受艾諾維斯公司的錄用。
Janet Nixon is ------------------------ the job offer from Inovis, Inc.

5 「領導都市公司」將要展開一項都市更新專案。
The Lead City Corporation is ------------------------ a city renovation project.

STEP 3 試題演練

請選出最適合填入空格的字詞。

1 The seminar room is big enough ------- a hundred participants.
(A) accommodate
(B) accommodation
(C) accommodating
(D) to accommodate

2 The finance manager is hesitant ------- in the Russian market because of the high risk.
(A) investment
(B) to invest
(C) has invested
(D) will invest

3 The New York office is too noisy ------- to concentrate on our work.
(A) us
(B) for us
(C) we
(D) to us

4 Intra Technology is scheduled ------- new security services in the Middle East.
(A) start
(B) to start
(C) starting
(D) to be started

多益實戰詞彙 片語動詞（1）

A 請熟記下列的高頻率片語動詞。

attend to a client 款待客戶	make a complaint 提出申訴
be accompanied by 由……陪伴	make a move 有所行動
be committed to 致力於……	obsess about 執著於……
bring up 提起（議題等）	post a notice on 張貼（某主題）的相關公告
carry out 執行……	provide A with B 向 A 提供 B
call off 取消……	put off 延期
compare A with B 將 A 和 B 做比較	refer to 參考……
compare A to B 將 A 和 B 做比較、將 A 比喻為 B	respond to 回應……
comply with 遵守……	result in (= cause) 造成……
convict A of B 因為 B 將 A 定罪	specialize in 專精於……
cut back on costs 縮減成本	sign up for 報名參加……
distinguish A from B 區分 A 和 B 的差異	shut down 倒閉、關閉
draw up 草擬（文件等）	take charge of 收取……的費用
file for bankruptcy 申請破產	transfer A to B 將 A 轉調到 B 地／B 部門
give away 贈送……、捐出……	turn in 呈交……
let down 辜負……、使……失望	take action 採取行動
look forward to 期待……	turn to 轉而……

B 請選出與中文意思相符的詞彙。

1 令專案經理失望 → (let / send) down the project coordinator

2 捐出舊的辦公室設備 → (turn / give) away the old office equipment

3 減少購物 → (put / cut) back on shopping

4 將米勒先生調到大阪辦公室 → (transfer / waive) Mr. Miller to the Osaka office

5 報名參加線上課程 → (sign / enroll) up for the online course

6 延後預算會議 → (call / put) off the budget meeting

7 草擬新的協議 → (turn / draw) up a new agreement

8 提起敏感議題 → (come / bring) up a sensitive issue

9 遵守政府政策 → (comply / lead) with government policies

10 造成財務困難 → (result / cause) in financial difficulty

Practice Test 實戰演練

Part 5 請選出最適合填入空格的字詞。

1. The purpose of the orientation is ------- new engineers understand how to operate the new devices efficiently.

   (A) for help
   (B) to help
   (C) helped
   (D) being helped

2. If you would like to use a conference room in March, be sure ------- one in advance.

   (A) book
   (B) to book
   (C) booking
   (D) for booking

3. Most of the staff members working on the second floor of the community center ------- in the care of children.

   (A) commit
   (B) belong
   (C) arrive
   (D) specialize

4. The plan to ------- the old city hall building into a community sports facility has been postponed.

   (A) changing
   (B) changes
   (C) change
   (D) be changed

5. If you are interested in applying to Samson, Inc., ------- to the company's website for further information.

   (A) refer
   (B) to refer
   (C) reference
   (D) referring

6. Most of the major companies are ------- to hire more employees because they are experiencing financial difficulties.

   (A) hesitant
   (B) hesitation
   (C) hesitated
   (D) be hesitated

7. Ms. Williams has successfully ------- the tasks outlined in her contract.

   (A) carried out
   (B) met
   (C) strived
   (D) called for

8. ------- the use of artificial intelligence, the government provides researchers with a significant amount of funds.

   (A) Promotion
   (B) To be promoted
   (C) For promoting
   (D) To promote

9. When picking up a press pass, journalists need ------- proof of identification to the receptionist.

(A) show
(B) to show
(C) showing
(D) to be shown

10. All employees should contact their immediate supervisors if they expect ------- to work late.

(A) comes
(B) coming
(C) will come
(D) to come

11. Mr. Wood is in charge of handling the changes that are about ------- in the Production Department.

(A) happen
(B) happenings
(C) happening
(D) to happen

12. The project manager has decided to ------- the meeting with the suppliers.

(A) raise
(B) call off
(C) specialize
(D) remind

13. The Management Department will ------- a notice on the backup power plan in the event of a power failure.

(A) reply
(B) post
(C) refer
(D) lead

14. ------- increase efficiency and productivity, we need to obtain state-of-the-art manufacturing systems.

(A) If
(B) Because
(C) In order to
(D) So

15. The board of directors believes that Ms. Freeman is talented enough ------- the executive position.

(A) handle
(B) handles
(C) to handle
(D) handling

16. Mr. Mondi asked a junior member of the staff ------- all the terms and conditions by this week.

(A) look over
(B) looked over
(C) has looked over
(D) to look over

Practice Test

Part 6 請先閱讀文章，再選出適合填入空格的內容。

Questions 17-20 refer to the following advertisement.

Job Opening at Reynolds Telecom

The Customer Service Department at Reynolds Telecom is looking for people who can fill several bilingual customer service representative positions. Your responsibilities will include helping customers in both English ------- (**17.**) your language of expertise with accounts and billing issues. ------- (**18.**). Specific technical terms will be covered during the job-training process.

Applicants should have native-level English skills and near-native ------- (**19.**) in one of the following languages: Spanish, Turkish, Japanese, Korean, Chinese, or Hungarian. Additionally, you must be a college graduate ------- (**20.**) for this job. Please visit our website at www.reytel.com/careers for more information.

17. (A) or
(B) and
(C) but
(D) nor

18. (A) If you are interested, please submit an application.
(B) New hires will be given three weeks of paid training to prepare for the job.
(C) Customers need to provide their contact information to receive help.
(D) We are always looking for skilled individuals to work at our company.

19. (A) interest
(B) opportunity
(C) proficiency
(D) certification

20. (A) qualify
(B) qualifies
(C) to qualify
(D) for qualifying

Part 7 請閱讀文章，並選出正確答案。

Questions 21-24 refer to the following online chat discussion.

Larai Igbokwe [9:01 a.m.]

Thank you, everyone, for making time to get together online this morning. There are a few quick things I'd like to discuss for the new exhibition opening next month. I want to make sure that this event runs smoothly in order to maintain our hotel's reputation. Celine, have you made the catering arrangements for the opening day?

Celine DeVoe [9:01 a.m.]

Yes, Sutherland Caterers will arrive by noon to set up and prepare for the event.

Larai Igbokwe [9:02 a.m.]

Perfect. They can set up in the main hall. Nick, can you put together a team to help them set up? Maybe some of the part-timers can help.

Nick Keys [9:03 a.m.]

Sure. How many people do you think we'll need?

Larai Igbokwe [9:04 a.m.]

I think 5 or 6 should be enough. What do you think, Celine?

Celine DeVoe [9:04 a.m.]

That should do it.

Nick Keys [9:05 a.m.]

Okay, then I'll send out some emails after the meeting.

Larai Igbokwe [9:05 a.m.]

Good. Moving on, we need to figure out a solution for additional parking.

Celine DeVoe [9:06 a.m.]

Right. We don't want people to wait for spaces.

Send

Practice Test

21. What is the online chat discussion mainly about?

(A) Choosing a venue

(B) Organizing a company event

(C) Changing a supplier

(D) Hiring new part-timers

22. Where most likely do the writers work?

(A) At a law firm

(B) At a museum

(C) At an IT company

(D) At a hotel

23. At 9:04 a.m., what does Ms. DeVoe most likely mean when she writes, "That should do it"?

(A) She agrees with Ms. Igbokwe.

(B) The staff members should help out.

(C) They should hire more part-timers.

(D) The catering is a good idea.

24. What will Mr. Keys do next?

(A) Reschedule an arrangement

(B) Contact part-time workers

(C) Install a machine

(D) Extend a parking lot

Unit 4

動名詞

Gerunds

01 動名詞的角色和特色

02 連接動名詞作為受詞的動詞

03 動名詞的慣用語

★ 多益實戰詞彙：片語動詞（2）

★ 實戰演練

Unit 4

01 動名詞的角色和特色

STEP 1 題型觀摩

Q ------- coupon books on a regular basis is a good way to encourage customers to spend more money in the store.

(A) Offer
(B) Offers
(C) Offering
(D) Offered

Q 定期主動發送禮券本，是鼓勵顧客到店多消費的好方法。

(A) 主動發送（名詞；原形動詞、現在簡單式）
(B) 主動發送（現在簡單式〔第三人稱單數〕）
(C) 主動發送（現在分詞、動名詞）
(D)（被）主動發送（過去簡單式、過去分詞）

答案 (C)

本題考點為「動名詞當主詞」。本題同時列出名詞（Offer）和動名詞（Offering），要求從中選出適當的答案。名詞後面要加上介系詞，才能再連接一個名詞；**而動名詞本身具備動詞的性質，因此後面可以直接連接名詞**，故答案為 (C)。

1 動名詞的角色

作為主詞	**Dealing** with customer complaints is not an easy job to do. 處理客訴並不是一件簡單的工作。〔dealing ＝主詞〕
作為動詞的受詞	Employees do not enjoy **working** extra hours, even with overtime pay. 即使有加班費，員工仍不喜歡加班。〔working ＝動詞的受詞〕
作為主詞補語或受詞補語	What the consultant suggested is gradually **introducing** a new system. 顧問所建議的，是逐步引進新制度。〔introducing ＝主詞補語〕 The interviewer kept me **waiting** for 30 minutes without any notice. 面試官沒有事先通知，而讓我等了 30 分鐘。〔waiting ＝受詞補語〕
作為介系詞的受詞	In spite of **feeling** sick, Mr. Evans has decided not to cancel his business trip. 儘管身體不適，伊凡斯先生還是決定不取消出差。〔feeling ＝介系詞的受詞〕

2 動名詞的特色

(1) 可以直接連接受詞。

Understanding (動名詞) **students' needs** (受詞) will help you manage your class more effectively.

了解學生的需求能幫助你更有效地管理班級。

(2) 可以用副詞修飾。

The company is devoted to **promptly** (副詞) **providing** (動名詞) all types of media technology.

這家公司致力於迅速提供各類媒體科技。

STEP 2 文法練習

請參考句子的中文意思，從提示字詞中選出適當的動詞後，改寫成正確的動名詞形態填入空格，並選出該動名詞扮演的角色為何。

提示	use	maximize	make	keep	take

1 研發團隊提議逐步更改付款方式。
The R&D team suggested ________________ gradual changes in the payment methods.
(主詞｜動詞的受詞｜主詞補語或受詞補語｜介系詞的受詞)

2 顧客滿意度最大化是我們的重要目標之一。
________________ customers' satisfaction is one of our important goals.
(主詞｜動詞的受詞｜主詞補語或受詞補語｜介系詞的受詞)

3 我們應試著避免使用塑料，才能保護環境。
We should try to avoid ________________ plastic materials in order to protect the environment.
(主詞｜動詞的受詞｜主詞補語或受詞補語｜介系詞的受詞)

4 請避免在週一和週五請假。
Please refrain from ________________ a day off on Mondays and Fridays.
(主詞｜動詞的受詞｜主詞補語或受詞補語｜介系詞的受詞)

STEP 3 試題演練

請選出最適合填入空格的字詞。

1 Thank you for ------- to travel with City Pass, which we created 30 years ago to provide the best vacation experience.

(A) choose
(B) choosing
(C) to choose
(D) choice

2 ------- workers with appropriate rewards will help motivate them.

(A) Provide
(B) Providing
(C) Provision
(D) To be provided

3 We will discuss some effective ways of ------- clients' needs to the greatest possible extent.

(A) meet
(B) meets
(C) to meet
(D) meeting

4 By ------- this contract, you will be eligible for all the benefits we are offering.

(A) sign
(B) to sign
(C) signing
(D) signed

02 連接動名詞作為受詞的動詞

STEP 1 題型觀摩

Q The marketing team will consider ------- a new promotional campaign this coming month.

(A) start
(B) to start
(C) starting
(D) starts

Q 行銷團隊將考慮在下個月展開新的促銷宣傳活動。

(A) 展開（原形動詞、現在簡單式）
(B) 展開（不定詞 to V）
(C) 展開（現在分詞、動名詞）
(D) 展開（現在簡單式〔第三人稱單數〕）

答案 (C)

命題重點 動詞 consider（考慮）後面要連接動名詞作為受詞，因此答案為動名詞 (C) starting。動名詞考題中經常出現此種考題類型，因此請把後面要連接動名詞的動詞一併熟記。

1 連接動名詞作為受詞的動詞

mind 介意	consider 考慮	quit 退出、停止	enjoy 享受
avoid 避免	finish 完成	admit 承認	recommend 推薦、建議
risk 冒險	deny 否認	keep 保持	practice 練習
miss 逃過、錯失	imagine 想像	delay 延遲	risk 冒險
include 包括	suggest 提議	give up 放棄	postpone 延期

Passengers should **avoid** moving around when the vehicle is on the move.
乘客應避免於行車時走動。

Visitors to this beach can now **enjoy** having snacks while they are swimming.
此海灘的遊客現在可享受一邊游泳一邊吃零食的樂趣。

2 能連接動名詞，也能連接不定詞 to V 作為受詞的動詞

兩者意思相同	兩者意思不同
start to V / V-ing 開始做某事 begin to V / V-ing 開始做某事 continue to V / V-ing 繼續做某事 bother to V / V-ing 勞煩自己去做某事	forget to V 忘記去做某事（未做） forget V-ing 忘記做過某事（已做） remember to V 記得去做某事（未做） remember V-ing 記得做過某事（已做） stop to V 停止手邊動作改做某事（未做） stop V-ing 停止做某事（正在做） regret to V 很遺憾做某事（正要做） regret V-ing 後悔做過某事（已做） try to V 努力嘗試做某件（困難的）事 try V-ing 試試看做某件（簡單的）事

The computer manufacturer **began** to expand / expanding into electric appliance industry.
這家電腦製造商開始將版圖拓展至電器用品產業。

We **regret** to inform you that the service you requested is no longer available.
我們很遺憾地通知您，您要求的服務已不存在。

STEP 2 文法練習

請參考句子的中文意思，從提示字詞中選出兩個適當的動詞後，改寫成正確的形態填入空格中。

提示	admit	include	make	hold
	postpone	submit	stop	complain

1 財務經理的職責，包含做出與開支相關的重要決策。
The finance manager's duties ________ ________ important decisions about expenditures.

2 如果你想減低人生的悲慘程度，就應該停止抱怨。
You should ________ ________ if you want to make your life less miserable.

3 他們將把年度嘉年華會延至夏季舉行。
They will ________ ________ the annual festival until summer.

4 這位應徵者承認交出假的學歷資料。
The applicant ________ ________ wrong information about his educational background.

STEP 3 試題演練

請選出最適合填入空格的字詞。

1 The company is considering ------- a new logo to celebrate its 20th anniversary.
(A) make
(B) making
(C) makes
(D) made

2 The company regretted ------- a high-end watch when the economic situation was not so favorable.
(A) launch
(B) launching
(C) to launch
(D) to be launched

3 We recommend ------- public parking since our parking structure is currently being renovated.
(A) use
(B) usage
(C) using
(D) user

4 The store decided to quit ------- customers with free gifts when they make a purchase of over 200 dollars.
(A) provision
(B) provided
(C) provider
(D) providing

Unit 4

03 動名詞的慣用語

STEP 1 題型觀摩

Q We look forward to ------- with you in the near future.	Q 我們期待在不久的將來與您合作。
(A) work	(A) 工作（名詞；原形動詞、現在簡單式）
(B) working	(B) 工作（現在分詞、動名詞）
(C) worked	(C) 工作（過去簡單式、過去分詞）
(D) worker	(D) 工作者（名詞）
	答案 (B)

「look forward to」（期待……）的 to 為介系詞，後面只能連接名詞或動名詞，而「work with you」的 work 須為動詞，才能表達「與您合作」的意思，故答案為動名詞 (B)。請熟記這一類搭配動名詞使用的慣用語，並特別注意搭配介系詞 to 使用的慣用語。

1 動名詞的慣用語

feel like V-ing 想做（某事）	cannot help V-ing 忍不住做（某事）
be busy V-ing 忙於做（某事）	go on V-ing 繼續做（某事）
have trouble/difficulty V-ing 在做（某事）方面有障礙／困難	it is no use V-ing 做（某事）是沒有用的
have a problem V-ing 在做（某事）方面遇到問題	be worth V-ing 值得做（某事）
have a hard time V-ing 在做（某事）方面不太順利	spend time/money V-ing 花時間／金錢做（某事）

This year's employee workshop is definitely **worth** signing up for.
今年的員工工作坊絕對值得報名參加。

Everybody **is busy** preparing for the company banquet.
每個人都忙著準備公司的宴會。

2 搭配介系詞 to 使用的動名詞慣用語

以下動名詞慣用語後面只能連接名詞或動名詞。

object to 反對……	be/get used to 習慣……
be committed to 致力於……	contribute to 造成……
be devoted to 致力於……	lead to 造成……
be addicted to 對……上癮	prior to 在……之前
look forward to 期待……	be opposed to 與……相反、反對……
be entitled to 享有……的資格／權力	be related to 與……有關

I **am** not completely **opposed to** shutting down the branch in Europe.
我並非完全反對關閉歐洲分公司。

Most of the staff members **are** not **used to** punching in and out.
大部分職員並不習慣上下班打卡。

STEP 2 文法練習

請參考句子的中文意思，從提示字詞中選出適當的慣用語後，改寫成正確的形態填入空格中。

提示			
	object to	be used to	go on
	be committed to	be related to	have difficulty

1 我們致力於為社區成員提供終身教育計畫。
We ________________ providing lifelong educational programs for community members.

2 最近顧客人數增加的原因，與新推出的電視廣告影片有關。
The recent increase in the number of customers ________________ launching a new TV commercial.

3 似乎沒有人反對引進新的員工考核制度。
No one seems to ________________ introducing a new employee evaluation system.

4 這間博物館似乎在夏季吸引更多來館者一事上碰到了困難。
The museum appears to ________________ attracting more visitors in the summer.

STEP 3 試題演練

請選出最適合填入空格的字詞。

1 After completing this training course, Mr. Evans will be in charge of ------- the CS team.

(A) supervise
(B) supervising
(C) supervisor
(D) supervision

2 Startup companies often have difficulty ------- experienced and competent employees.

(A) recruit
(B) recruiting
(C) recruitment
(D) to be recruited

3 We ask that everyone go through the security checkpoint prior ------- entering this building.

(A) of
(B) in
(C) from
(D) to

4 It would not be a good idea to spend too much time ------- private phone calls at work.

(A) made
(B) making
(C) to making
(D) will make

多益實戰詞彙　片語動詞（2）

A 請熟記下列的高頻率片語動詞。

benefit from 從……中受益	account for 說明……、占（某比例）
result from 肇因於……	succeed in 在……成功
result in 造成……	congratulate A on B 恭喜 A 在 B 方面的表現
dispose of 處置……	draw on 取材於……、引用……
deal with 處理……、應對……	take advantage of 利用……
contribute to 造成……、對……有所貢獻	go through 經歷……
pay for 支付……的金額	look over 查看……
compensate for 彌補……	back up 備份……
interfere with 干擾……	set aside 另外撥出……
prevent A from B 防止 A 受到 B 的影響	make up for 彌補……
engage in 參與……	do . . . good 對……有好處
register for 註冊……、報名參加……	come to an agreement (= reach an agreement) 達成協議
apply for ＋職位／工作 應徵職位／工作	refer to 參考……
apply to ＋公司 應徵公司	reply to 回應……
participate in 參與……	subscribe to 訂閱……、訂購……
take part in 參與……	comply with 遵守……

B 請選出與中文意思相符的詞彙。

1 達成協議 → (refer / come to) an agreement

2 彌補錯誤 → (make up / make in) for a mistake

3 引用之前的研究 → (take / draw) on previous research

4 支付學費 → (compensate for / pay for) school

5 對發展有所貢獻 → (attribute / contribute) to the development

6 參與討論 → (involve / engage) in a discussion

7 遵守規則 → (deal / comply) with rules

8 造成銷售量增加 → result (in / from) an increase in sales

9 回應顧客的需求 → reply (with / to) customers' needs

10 報名參加課程 → (apply / register) for a course

Practice Test 實戰演練

Part 5 請選出最適合填入空格的字詞。

1. We are so grateful to you for ------- time to participate in this survey.

   (A) take
   (B) took
   (C) taking
   (D) to take

2. With a 20% decrease in the workforce, the company is now ------- dramatic changes.

   (A) looking over
   (B) going through
   (C) doing good
   (D) replying to

3. If you would like to travel more frequently after retirement, you need to set ------- some funds for yourself.

   (A) for
   (B) from
   (C) in
   (D) aside

4. You should fill out this application form ------- to signing up for the workshop.

   (A) before
   (B) prior
   (C) advance
   (D) in front

5. If the item you have purchased does not work properly, you may want to ------- to the manual provided.

   (A) relate
   (B) refer
   (C) deal
   (D) engage

6. Paul's job as the leader of the R&D team includes ------- a great deal of research and practical testing.

   (A) do
   (B) doing
   (C) does
   (D) to do

7. I would like you to start by ------- the employee handbook thoroughly.

   (A) review
   (B) reviewing
   (C) reviewer
   (D) be reviewed

8. ------- for the overseas manager position must speak fluent English and have at least 3 years of experience.

   (A) Apply
   (B) Applying
   (C) Applicants
   (D) Applications

9. You cannot imagine ------- in a world where there are no Wi-Fi connections.

(A) live
(B) to live
(C) living
(D) to have lived

10. Anyone interested in subscribing ------- the *Daily Economic Journal* should leave their contact information on the website.

(A) with
(B) to
(C) from
(D) by

11. It is considered rude to keep your client ------- for more than 30 minutes.

(A) wait
(B) waiting
(C) be waited
(D) being waited

12. Mega Pharmaceuticals has succeeded in ------- a new medicine for people who suffer from insomnia.

(A) develop
(B) development
(C) developing
(D) developed

13. ------- for free online courses requires prompt action.

(A) Register
(B) Registrations
(C) Registering
(D) Registered

14. In order to avoid ------- too much money, you had better make a shopping list before going out.

(A) spending
(B) spent
(C) having spent
(D) being spent

15. Mr. Takahashi is ------- to a refund for last month's overcharges.

(A) entitled
(B) able
(C) capable
(D) likely

16. The doctor recommended ------- in group counseling so that the patient could get ideas and opinions from different perspectives.

(A) participating
(B) taking
(C) contributing
(D) restricting

Part 6 請先閱讀文章，再選出適合填入空格的內容。

Questions 17-20 refer to the following article.

JOPLIN (November 12) — The Regional Transportation Services Department has finally received -------**17.** to build a new bus terminal at the corner of Main Street and 15th Avenue. The terminal will expand service to the north side of Joplin, and it will act as a hub for intercity routes. Construction should begin on the third of next month.

Many commuters are excited about the city -------**18.** the new terminal, especially because it will bring 60 permanent jobs to the area. However, not everyone is excited about the expansion.

-------**19.** Jim Hurtz, a local resident, says, "Commuting every morning is already bad enough without more buses to share the road with. I'm sure the terminal will make things even more -------**20.**."

17. (A) approve
(B) approving
(C) approval
(D) approved

18. (A) build
(B) builds
(C) builder
(D) building

19. (A) The new routes will be free of charge for local residents.
(B) Many people think the construction will be expensive.
(C) Funding for the project has been delayed for several months.
(D) Many residents are worried about the terminal causing more traffic problems.

20. (A) sophisticated
(B) congested
(C) exceptional
(D) affordable

Part 7 請閱讀文章，並選出正確答案。

Questions 21-22 refer to the following memo.

MEMO

To: Sherry's Department Store General Floor Staff

From: Dave Wilcox, Senior HR Specialist

Re: New General Floor Manager

Date: February 15

This Wednesday, February 17, our new general floor manager, Jasmine Garcia, will be joining our team. As you may have heard, she is transferring here from the Springfield store, where she has worked for over 12 years, so she is new to St. Louis. She will be taking a tour of the floor from 9:00-11:00 a.m., so please introduce yourself if you have the chance and show her around your storefront. We will have a more formal meeting with Mrs. Garcia on Thursday morning at 8:00 a.m., where she will tell you more about herself and her plans for expanding the store and improving sales. As such, don't worry about asking her too many work-related details. Instead, let's just focus on trying to make her feel welcome on her first day here.

21. What is NOT indicated about Mrs. Garcia?

(A) She used to work at another branch of the company.

(B) She is going to have a meeting on Wednesday.

(C) She has plans to improve sales.

(D) She has worked for the company for more than 12 years.

22. What are the employees asked to do on February 17?

(A) Clean up their storefronts

(B) Attend a meeting

(C) Find out about the new manager's business plans

(D) Make the new general floor manager feel welcome

Unit 5

分詞

Participles

01 分詞的角色／須注意的分詞

02 分詞的慣用語

03 分詞構句

★ 多益實戰詞彙：片語動詞 (3)

★ 實戰演練

Unit 5

01 分詞的角色／須注意的分詞

STEP 1 題型觀摩

Q The internship program that Angela participated in at the local station made her ------- in the broadcasting industry. (A) interest (B) interesting (C) interested (D) has interested	**Q** 安琪拉在當地電台參加的實習課程，讓她對廣播業產生興趣。 (A) 使感興趣（原形動詞、現在簡單式） (B) 有趣的（現在分詞） (C) 感興趣的（過去分詞） (D) 已使感興趣（現在完成式〔第三人稱單數〕） 答案 (C)

命題重點 本題考的是是否能夠**區分現在分詞和過去分詞的差異**。空格要填入受詞補語，而受詞 her（她）為人，使用過去分詞 interested（感興趣的）時，後面的「in ＋名詞」表達「感興趣的對象」，意思完整，故答案為 (C)。現在分詞 interesting（有趣的）與題意不符，故不能作為答案。

1 現在分詞（V-ing）與過去分詞（p.p.）

分詞和其修飾的名詞之間屬於**主動關係**時，要用**現在分詞**；兩者屬於**被動關係**時，則用**過去分詞**。

The Sam & Heger Group is a **leading company** in engineering.〔在前領導的企業〕
山姆海格集團堪稱工程方面的佼佼者。

The usher in the theater guided us to our **reserved seats**.〔被預約的座位〕
電影院的帶位人員引導我們前往我們預訂的座位。

2 分詞扮演形容詞的角色

分詞和形容詞一樣，可以用來**修飾名詞**，也可以**當作主詞補語或受詞補語使用**，補充說明主詞或受詞。

The **presentation made** by Mr. Kim pointed out the **challenging tasks**.
〔放在名詞前方或後方作修飾〕
金先生所做的簡報，指出了具有挑戰性的任務項目。

The company was **pleased** with the outcome of the meeting.〔主詞補語〕
公司對於會議結果感到很滿意。

Critics found **the new play** very **amusing**.〔受詞補語〕
影評認為這場新劇非常逗趣。

3 表達情緒的分詞用法

interest、surprise 等表達情緒的及物動詞有兩種用法。若受修飾者為**引發情緒的對象（通常為事物）**時，要使用**現在分詞**；表達**感受到的情緒（通常為人）**時，則要使用**過去分詞**。

interesting 有趣的	interested 感興趣的	encouraging 激勵人心的	encouraged 受到鼓舞的
surprising 令人驚訝的	surprised 感到驚訝的	pleasing 令人開心的	pleased 感到開心的
fascinating 吸引人的	fascinated 極感興趣的	satisfying 令人滿足的	satisfied 感到滿足的

The new line of jeans from H&N was **disappointing**.〔引發的情緒〕
H&N 推出的新牛仔褲系列令人感到失望。

We were **disappointed** with the cancelation of our trip.〔感受到的情緒〕
我們對於旅遊行程取消一事感到很失望。

STEP 2 文法練習

請參考句子的中文意思，從提示字詞中選出適當的動詞後，改寫成現在分詞或過去分詞填入空格中。

提示	fascinate	satisfy	write	disappoint	inspire

1 我們覺得新手機的設計很吸引人。
We found the new cell phone's design ________________.

2 這場攝影展十分激勵人心。
The exhibition of photographs was really ________________.

3 員工對於加薪雙位數的待遇感到滿意。
The employees were ________________ with the double-figure pay raise.

4 你無法輕易違背紙本合約書的內容。
You cannot break a ________________ agreement easily.

5 新職員的工作表現令人失望。
The new staff member's work performance was ________________.

STEP 3 試題演練

請選出最適合填入空格的字詞。

1 Steven Price hired someone who is ------- and intelligent to run the company with him.

(A) talent
(B) to talent
(C) talented
(D) talents

2 We are very ------- to tell you that your employment contract has been extended for another two years.

(A) please
(B) pleased
(C) pleasing
(D) pleasure

3 The Valley Hotel is offering a special discount to its premium members for a ------- time.

(A) limiting
(B) limited
(C) limit
(D) limitation

4 From the investor's perspective, the merger of the two companies is not -------.

(A) surprising
(B) surprised
(C) surprise
(D) to be surprised

02 分詞的慣用語

STEP 1 題型觀摩

Q The best way to deal with a ------- supervisor is to accept the requests first and to negotiate a solution later. (A) demand (B) demands (C) demanding (D) demanded	**Q** 應對要求嚴苛的主管時，最好的辦法就是先接受要求，再協商解決方案。 (A) 要求（原形動詞、現在簡單式；名詞） (B) 要求（現在簡單式〔第三人稱單數〕） (C) 要求嚴苛的（現在分詞） (D) 被要求的（過去分詞） 答案 (C)

命題重點 「demanding supervisor」表示「要求嚴苛、難搞的上司」的意思，因此答案為 (C)。這類「分詞＋名詞」的慣用語經常出現在考題當中，若能一併熟記，將有助於解題。

1 現在分詞（V-ing）＋名詞

promising future 光明的前景	remaining seat 剩下的座位／席次
challenging work 具有挑戰性的工作	demanding supervisor 要求嚴苛的主管
inviting offer 吸引人的待遇	growing business 成長中的事業
misleading advertisement 誤導人的平面廣告	outstanding candidate 出色的候選人／應徵者
outstanding debt 未還債務	existing account 現有帳戶
surrounding area 周遭地區	increasing sales 增加中的業績
overwhelming support 壓倒性的支持	exciting opportunity 令人興奮的機會
	※outstanding 有「未支付的」及「出色的」兩個意思。

Online language programs have a very **promising future**.
線上語言課程的前景一片光明。

There are some **outstanding candidates** applying for the position.
有一些出色的應徵者來應徵這個職位。

2 過去分詞（p.p.）＋名詞

detailed information 詳細資訊	limited time 限時
approved proposal 受批准的提案	talented employee 有才華的員工
scheduled flight 預定班機	motivated staff 受到激勵的職員
reserved seat 預訂的座位	dedicated employee 盡心盡力的員工
anticipated profit 預期的利潤	established company 著名的公司
complicated issue 複雜的議題	qualified applicant 符合資格的應徵者
enclosed brochure 隨附的手冊	revised budget 修訂過的預算

JW International, Inc. is an **established company** with a sound reputation.
「JW 國際股份有限公司」為一家名聲可靠的著名公司。

STEP 2 文法練習

請參考句子的中文意思，從提示字詞中選出適當的分詞和名詞填入空格中。

提示					
	分詞：outstanding	qualified	complicated	detailed	surrounding
	名詞：areas	information	issue	applicant	debt

1 感謝您提供所有的詳細資訊。
Thank you for providing all your ________ ________.

2 這是一個十分複雜又敏感的議題。
It is a very ________ and sensitive ________.

3 我聽說拉金先生是資格最為符合的應徵者。
I heard that Mr. Larkin is the most ________ ________.

4 您的帳戶仍有 5000 美元的未還債務。
Your account has an ________ ________ of $5,000.

5 這個村莊與周遭地區都遇到了水患。
The villages and ________ ________ were flooded.

STEP 3 試題演練

請選出最適合填入空格的字詞。

1 The finance career fair is an ------- opportunity for college graduates to meet with recruiters.

(A) excite
(B) exciting
(C) excited
(D) excitement

2 Please take a look at the ------- brochure for benefits that you can receive as a premium subscriber.

(A) enclosed
(B) enclosing
(C) encloses
(D) enclose

3 I would like to pay tribute to the ------- employees of Canadian Rail, who worked hard to provide better service.

(A) dedicate
(B) dedicating
(C) dedicated
(D) dedication

4 If you have an ------- email account with us and want to open another one, please email us for assistance.

(A) exist
(B) existed
(C) existing
(D) existence

03 分詞構句

STEP 1 題型觀摩

Q ------- $200 worth of groceries between now and December 10, shoppers will receive a free gift card.

(A) Purchase
(B) Purchases
(C) Purchased
(D) Purchasing

Q 從現在開始至 12 月 10 日止，顧客只要購買價值 200 美元的生活雜貨用品，即可獲得一張免費的禮品卡。

(A) 購買（原形動詞、現在簡單式；名詞）
(B) 購買（現在簡單式〔第三人稱單數〕）
(C)（被）購買（過去簡單式、過去分詞）
(D) 購買（現在分詞、動名詞）

答案 (D)

命題重點 本題屬於典型的分詞構句考題，空格置於句首，其句子後面又出現一個子句。根據題意，使用**主動語態**來表達「顧客『購買』生活雜貨用品」較為適當，因此答案要使用**現在分詞 V-ing** 的形態，故選 (D)。

1 副詞子句簡化成分詞構句

將副詞子句中的**連接詞和主詞省略**後，於**動詞後面加上** -ing，便是分詞構句。表示條件、時間、讓步、原因等意思的連接詞都可以省略。

簡化成分詞構句的步驟
❶ 省略連接詞
❷ 省略主詞（僅限於與主要子句的主詞一致時）
❸ 動詞後面加上 -ing（being 可省略）

(1) **現在分詞**開頭的分詞構句（表示**主動**）

~~If you~~ sign up for a membership, you will get a 10% discount on all items.
→ **Signing** up for a membership, you will get a 10% discount on all items.
若你註冊加入會員，即可擁有全品項九折的優惠。

(2) **過去分詞**開頭的分詞構句（表示**被動**）

~~Because Mr. Choi~~ was unemployed for a couple of years, **he** could not afford to pay the rent.
→ **(Being) Unemployed** for a couple of years, Mr. Choi could not afford to pay the rent.
因為崔先生好幾年沒有工作，故無法負擔租金。

2 完成式分詞構句（表示動作更早完成）

副詞子句的動作比主要子句的動作更早完成時，動詞要使用「having + p.p.」的形態。

~~After I~~ wrote a letter of complaint, I received a reply from the company.
→ **Having written** a letter of complaint, I received a reply from the company.
我寫了投訴信之後，收到了該公司的回應。

STEP 2 文法練習

請參考句子的中文意思，從提示字詞中選出適當的分詞填入空格中。

提示	working	disappointed	conducting	having completed	turning

1 費里曼先生完成艱難的專案後，去了夏威夷度假。
_______________ a tough project, Mr. Freeman went on vacation to Hawaii.

2 全先生對管理階層感到失望，跳槽去了別家公司。
_______________ by management, Mr. Quan moved to a different company.

3 米爾斯先生進行了許多市場研究，對顧客知之甚深。
_______________ lots of market research, Mr. Mills learned a lot about customers.

4 洪先生身為銀行家，努力追求金額上的準確度。
_______________ as a banker, Mr. Hong tried hard to be accurate with money.

5 在街角左轉後，你很容易就能找到自然史博物館。
_______________ left at the corner, you will easily find the museum of natural history.

STEP 3 試題演練

請選出最適合填入空格的字詞。

1 ------- working abroad, Ms. Swan desired to emigrate to a foreign country.

(A) Having experienced
(B) To experience
(C) Being experienced
(D) Experience

2 ------- mathematics in college, Ms. Kim is now working as an analyst at a finance company.

(A) Studied
(B) Having studied
(C) Being studied
(D) To study

3 ------- in the center of the city, the Seoul Hotel is the best place to hold an awards ceremony.

(A) Located
(B) Locating
(C) Locate
(D) Location

4 ------- the best salesperson of the year, Ms. Rolling was rewarded with a cash bonus.

(A) Select
(B) Selecting
(C) Being selected
(D) Selection

多益實戰詞彙 片語動詞（3）

A 請熟記下列的高頻率片語動詞。

turn off 關閉（電器）	depend on 依賴（某人）、依（某事）而定
break down 故障	interact with 與……互動
look around 環顧四周	agree on 對……有共識
set up 建立……、設置……	focus on 專注於……
go through 經歷……	vote for 針對……來表決
touch down 著陸	succeed in 在……成功
narrow down 縮小……的範圍	subscribe to 訂閱……、訂購……
pick up 拾起（某物）、接（某人）	account for 說明……、占（某比例）
look into 調查……	merge with 與……合併
let down 辜負……、使……失望	register for 報名……、註冊……
let in 允許……進入	participate in 參與……
benefit from 從……中受益	report to 向……呈報
consist of 由……組成	function as 具有……的功能
cooperate with 與……合作	contribute to 造成……、對……有貢獻
conflict with 與……有衝突	belong to 屬於……
remark on 評論（某事）	lead to 造成……
compete with 與……競爭	interfere with 干擾……

B 請選出與中文意思相符的詞彙。

1 從競爭中受益 → (result from / benefit from) the competition

2 由三個部分組成 → (belong to / consist of) three parts

3 與我的行程有衝突 → (conflict with / cooperate with) my schedule

4 事業成功 → (succeed in / lead to) business

5 視業績而定 → (depend on / comply with) sales

6 占我們收入的百分之 20 → (account for / consist of) 20 percent of our income

7 積極與人們互動 → actively (interfere with / interact with) people

8 對該建議有共識 → (agree on / let in) the suggestion

9 選出新的總監 → (vote for / search for) the new director

10 報名工作坊 → (register for / look into) the workshop

Practice Test 實戰演練

Part 5 請選出最適合填入空格的字詞。

1. Employees ------- in retiring early should contact Ms. Yang in the HR Department.

(A) interested
(B) interesting
(C) interest
(D) interests

2. The 3D printer is an ------- new development, and experts predict it will be available in our homes shortly.

(A) excite
(B) exciting
(C) excited
(D) excitement

3. ------- by well-known architect James King, I decided to work in the field of architecture.

(A) Inspiring
(B) Inspired
(C) Inspiration
(D) Inspire

4. Dr. Wang will give a presentation to attendees who are ------- about what to eat to stay healthy.

(A) confuse
(B) confused
(C) confusing
(D) confusion

5. Ms. Sherman ------- her supervisor down by not coming to work on time.

(A) paid
(B) saw
(C) let
(D) voted

6. Mr. Mille is working with highly ------- colleagues on a project to build a local sports complex.

(A) motivate
(B) motivation
(C) motivated
(D) motivating

7. Mr. Cho has been trying hard not to let work ------- his personal life.

(A) cooperate with
(B) interfere with
(C) succeed in
(D) deal with

8. ------- all the specifications, the quality inspectors gave their approval for the product to be released.

(A) To check
(B) Checked
(C) Having checked
(D) Having been checked

9. Local businesses such as clothing and furniture stores ------- big chain shops.

(A) comply with
(B) compete with
(C) belong to
(D) account for

10. ------- a financial crisis, management decided to close down the factory in L.A.

(A) Experience
(B) Experiencing
(C) Having experienced
(D) Experienced

11. Mr. Ozaki won the World Design Award because he had ------- support in an online poll.

(A) overwhelms
(B) overwhelmed
(C) overwhelming
(D) to overwhelm

12. As of August 1, all employees on the marketing team have to ------- Mr. Powell.

(A) function as
(B) vote for
(C) report to
(D) lead to

13. Quick Fix Repairs succeeded at ------- its sales by 40 percent in the first quarter.

(A) increase
(B) increasing
(C) increased
(D) being increased

14. The audience in the concert hall was ------- by the band's exceptional performance.

(A) fascinated
(B) fascinating
(C) to fascinate
(D) being fascinated

15. The high unemployment rate and rising interest rates ------- the economic crisis.

(A) specialized in
(B) contributed to
(C) qualified for
(D) relied on

16. The director of overseas marketing wrote a recommendation letter for Mr. Chen because he was a ------- and loyal employee.

(A) dedicate
(B) dedicated
(C) dedicating
(D) dedication

Practice Test

Part 6 請先閱讀文章，再選出適合填入空格的內容。

Questions 17-20 refer to the following announcement.

Announcing: The Pumpkin Festival

This year's festival ------- (**17.**) in the Wilson family's pumpkin patch this Saturday and Sunday, October 10-11. Guests at the festival will find a variety of family games to play and other activities, ------- (**18.**) face painting and live music. The festival will also feature a crafts market where members of the community will sell handmade products. As usual, all guests will be able to pick their own pumpkin from the pumpkin patch on both days of the festival. ------- (**19.**). Each pumpkin will be sold according to its weight. Are you ready to enjoy organically ------- (**20.**) pumpkins? Admission is free, so come early to get the best choice of pumpkins!

17. (A) held
(B) holds
(C) will hold
(D) will be held

18. (A) including
(B) included
(C) being included
(D) to include

19. (A) Pumpkins will not be sold to the general public.
(B) There is a limit of one pumpkin per guest.
(C) Pumpkin pie will only be sold from 12:00 p.m. to 2:00 p.m.
(D) Do not forget to bring a pumpkin from home to decorate.

20. (A) grow
(B) grows
(C) grown
(D) growing

Part 7 請閱讀文章，並選出正確答案。

Questions 21-23 refer to the following advertisement.

First National Bank

Newly Built South Hampton Location

Grand Opening: Monday, June 12

First National Bank has been a part of the community for over 20 years, and we are now expanding our service to the South Hampton area. Our newly built banking location will offer a wide variety of services, including:

- *Personal checking / savings*
- *Investment consultation & financial profile management*
- *Personalized business account management*
- *Drive-thru tellers & a 24-hour drive-thru ATM*

To celebrate our new location, any customer who opens a savings account and deposits at least $300 will receive a $50 bonus as a gift from us. In addition, we will be giving away free calendars to our first 250 guests on our opening day.

21. What is mentioned about First National Bank?

(A) It will be opening a new branch.
(B) It only handles personal banking.
(C) It has been relocated to South Hampton.
(D) It has not been in the area for very long.

22. What will be provided to customers who open new savings accounts?

(A) Cash
(B) Free counseling
(C) A higher interest rate
(D) A special investment opportunity

23. What service will NOT be provided at the new location?

(A) Customized account management
(B) A drive-thru ATM available any time of the day
(C) Financial profile management
(D) Free online banking

Unit 6

名詞

Nouns

01 名詞的角色和位置

02 可數名詞／不可數名詞

03 須注意的複合名詞

★ 多益實戰詞彙：人物／事物名詞 vs. 抽象名詞

★ 實戰演練

01 名詞的角色和位置

STEP 1 題型觀摩

Q An ------- to the new system will be given right after the presentation.

(A) introduce
(B) introducing
(C) introduction
(D) introductory

Q 簡報結束後，將立刻介紹新系統。

(A) 介紹（原形動詞、現在簡單式）
(B) 介紹（現在分詞、動名詞）
(C) 介紹（可數名詞〔單數〕）
(D) 入門的（形容詞）

答案 (C)

命題重點 本題將空格置於不定冠詞 an 的後面，應填入名詞，因此答案為 (C)。名詞可以在句子中扮演主詞的角色，通常會放在「冠詞／所有格（＋形容詞）」的後面。

1 名詞的角色

當作主詞		Your **request** has been received, and it will be processed promptly. 我們已受理您的要求，並將立即處理。
當作受詞	動詞的受詞	You should make a smart and quick **decision.** 你應該做出明智且即時的決定。
	介系詞的受詞	You can visit the website for additional **information.** 你可以前往網站了解更多資訊。
	不定詞的受詞	To replace some **parts,** refer to the manual provided. 如須更換部分零件，請參閱隨附的使用手冊。
	動名詞的受詞	One of her duties includes supervising an **accounting team.** 她的職責之一包括對會計團隊予以監督。
當作補語	主詞補語	Thomas Gibson is our new **chairman**. 湯瑪斯・吉布森是我們的新主席。
	受詞補語	The company appointed him a **floor manager**. 公司指派他擔任樓管。

2 名詞的位置

冠詞＋名詞	They are going to hire **an accountant**. 他們將僱用一位會計師。
所有格＋名詞	**My concern** is that we cannot afford to hire any new staffers. 我擔心的是我們沒錢僱用任何新職員。
冠詞／所有格＋形容詞＋名詞	We decided to film **a new commercial**. 我們決定拍攝一支新的商業廣告影片。

STEP 2 文法練習

將以下句子翻成中文，並寫出畫底線處名詞所扮演的角色為何。

1 They usually have a lot of information about employee welfare.
→〔中文翻譯〕____________.
→〔角　色〕information ____________ / employee welfare ____________

2 His suggestion about the recent crisis is considered appropriate.
→〔中文翻譯〕____________.
→〔角　色〕suggestion ____________ / crisis ____________

3 The lawyer doesn't think the candidate is qualified for the position.
→〔中文翻譯〕____________.
→〔角　色〕lawyer ____________ / candidate ____________

4 It was a great shock that we didn't get the deal signed.
→〔中文翻譯〕____________.
→〔角　色〕shock ____________ / deal ____________

STEP 3 試題演練

請選出最適合填入空格的字詞。

1 The order will be completed once your ------- is received.
(A) pay
(B) paying
(C) payment
(D) payer

2 The ------- of the working environment is a key to promoting productivity.
(A) improve
(B) improvement
(C) improving
(D) improved

3 The number of people who come to the city for ------- is rapidly going up.
(A) vacation
(B) vacate
(C) vacating
(D) vacancy

4 ------- for a scholarship often takes a lot of time and preparation.
(A) Apply
(B) Applying
(C) Applications
(D) Applicants

02 可數名詞／不可數名詞

STEP 1 題型觀摩

Q If you would like to get a work -------, you must have a bachelor's degree in a related field. (A) permit (B) permission (C) permits (D) permitting	Q 如果你想拿到工作許可證，就必須要有相關領域的學士學位。 (A) 許可證（可數名詞〔單數〕）、允許（原形動詞、現在簡單式） (B) 許可、權限（不可數名詞） (C) 許可證（可數名詞〔複數〕）、允許（現在簡單式〔第三人稱單數〕） (D) 允許（現在分詞、動名詞） 答案 (A)

命題重點 該類考題考的是**判斷空格內應填入可數名詞還是不可數名詞**。本題中，空格前方出現冠詞 a，這表示「work _____」為可數名詞。接著，(A) permit 和 (C) permits 都有可數名詞「許可證」的用法，但複數的 (C) 與表示單數的冠詞 a 不符，因此答案應選 (A)。

1 可數名詞和不可數名詞的特色

可數名詞	不可數名詞
單數形態不可單獨使用。 You need to place **order**. (X) You need to place an **order**. (O) 你必須下訂單。 單數形態要搭配冠詞或所有格一起使用。 I am looking for **key**. (X) I am looking for the **key**. (O) 我正在找（那把）鑰匙。 I am looking for my **key**. (O) 我正在找我的鑰匙。 複數形態可單獨使用。 We are thinking of hiring **consultants**. (O) 我們正在考慮聘請顧問。	可單獨使用，前面不用加上冠詞或所有格。但有必要時，可選擇搭配冠詞或所有格一起使用。 We will provide you with **information**. 我們會提供資訊給你。 The **information** you provided is wrong. 你提供的資訊是錯誤的。 沒有複數形態，只能使用單數形態，因此要搭配單數動詞一起使用。 Some **research** is necessary to find out more about it. 要深入了解這件事，有必要進行某些研究。

2 須注意的可數名詞／不可數名詞

請熟記下方意思或外型相似的可數名詞和不可數名詞。

可數名詞	不可數名詞	可數名詞	不可數名詞
a job 工作	work 工作	a bag 包包	baggage 行李
clothes 衣服〔複數〕	clothing 服飾	a tool 工具	equipment 設備
a view 景色、景觀	scenery 風景、景色	a certificate 證照	certification 認證
an accountant 會計師	accounting 會計（學）	a machine 機器	machinery 機械
an account 帳戶		a permit 許可證	permission 許可
a suggestion 建議	advice 建議	a survey 問卷調查	research 研究
a product 產品	merchandise 商品	a ticket 票券	ticketing 票務
goods 商品〔複數〕		a product 產品	productivity 產能
a chair 椅子	furniture 家具		

STEP 2 文法練習

請參考句子的中文意思，確認畫底線處的名詞前面是否需要加上冠詞。如有需要，請將冠詞填入括號中。

1 我的老闆要求所有職員都須對這件事提出建議。
My ( ) **boss** wanted all of the staff ( ) **members** to make ( ) **suggestion** about it.

2 這家旅行社將進行問卷調查，好了解潛在顧客需要什麼。
The ( ) **agency** will perform ( ) **survey** in order to find out what potential ( ) **customers** need.

3 這家店擁有您開業所需的豐富產品品項。
( ) **Store** has a wide variety of ( ) **products** that you need to run your ( ) **business**.

4 您可以從位於 25 樓的客房欣賞美景。
You can enjoy ( ) beautiful **view** from your ( ) **room** on the 25th floor.

5 如果您找不到您的行李，就必須先填寫表格。
If you can't find your ( ) **baggage**, you have to fill out ( ) **form** first.

6 你應該開立帳戶，才能把一些錢匯回你的母國。
You should open ( ) **account** to transfer some ( ) **money** to your home country.

STEP 3 試題演練

請選出最適合填入空格的字詞。

1 Although she was very interested in the job, she didn't have much experience in the field of -------.

(A) account
(B) accounts
(C) accountants
(D) accounting

2 At the upcoming workshop, we are supposed to discuss several ways to boost -------.

(A) product
(B) produce
(C) productivity
(D) producing

3 In order to park your car, you should obtain a parking -------.

(A) permit
(B) permitted
(C) permission
(D) to permit

4 A local consultant visited our office with some ------- to advertise our products to more people in the community.

(A) suggest
(B) suggested
(C) suggestion
(D) suggestions

03 須注意的複合名詞

STEP 1 題型觀摩

Q The national park is one of the major tourist ------- you shouldn't miss during your stay here. (A) attract (B) attracted (C) attraction (D) attractions	**Q** 這座國家公園是大家到此遊玩期間不可錯過的主要觀光景點之一。 (A) 吸引（原形動詞、現在簡單式） (B)（被）吸引（過去簡單式、過去分詞） (C) 景點（可數名詞〔單數〕） (D) 景點（可數名詞〔複數〕） 答案 (D)

命題重點 「tourist attraction」為複合名詞，意思為「觀光景點」。而名詞必須為複數，才能說「one of . . .」（……其中之一），因此答案為複數形態的 (D) attractions。多益測驗中，經常出現此類複合名詞的考題，請熟記下面所列出的複合名詞。

1 常見的複合名詞

safety regulations 安全規範	a board meeting 董事會議
a performance review 績效考核	an expiration date 到期日
a job interview 工作面試	office supplies 辦公用品
a job applicant 應徵工作者	a protective helmet 安全帽
sales figures 銷售數據	a tourist attraction 觀光景點
an job opening 職缺	an application deadline 申請截止日期
an application form 申請表	a construction worker 營建工人
a bank account 銀行帳戶	a construction site 工地
a work permit 工作許可證	a visitor's pass 訪客通行證
a job fair 公開徵才活動	a product review 產品評論
an account number 帳戶號碼	interest rates 利率
a return policy 退貨政策	a safety inspection 安全檢查

You can renew your membership at no extra charge if you call us before the **expiration date**.
如果您在到期日之前聯絡我們，更新會員資格就不需額外費用。

2 複合名詞的特徵

(1) **複合名詞（名詞＋名詞）被視為一個單字，置於前面的名詞扮演形容詞的角色。**

a **performance** **review** 績效考核〔與績效有關的考核〕
a **product** **review** 產品評論〔與產品有關的評論〕

(2) **動詞單複數**由**複合名詞後面的名詞**來決定。

Safety **regulations** **are** presented in the handbook.
複數名詞 複數動詞
手冊裡列有安全法規。

The construction **site** **is** located on 7th Avenue.
單數名詞 單數動詞
該工地位於第七大道上。

STEP 2 文法練習

請參考句子的中文意思，從提示字詞中選出適當的名詞填入空格中。

提示	supplies	openings	policy	deadline	visitor's	fair	program

1 在您決定退貨之前，請先詳讀我們的退貨規定。
Please read our return ______________ carefully before you decide to return your items.

2 如有任何職缺，我們會盡快通知您。
If there are any job ______________, we will let you know as soon as possible.

3 你能在我們提供的資料冊裡找到申請截止日的資訊。
You can find the application ______________ in the packet provided.

4 您必須取得訪客通行證，才能進出我們的設施。
You should obtain a ______________ pass in order to access one of our facilities.

5 我參加了一場公開徵才活動，某些公司有意錄用我。
I attended a job ______________, and some of the firms were interested in me.

6 我們會在網路上訂購一些辦公室用品，好獲得更划算的價格。
We will order some office ______________ online to get a better deal.

STEP 3 試題演練

請選出最適合填入空格的字詞。

1 A protective helmet should be worn at the ------- site at all times.

(A) construct
(B) constructing
(C) constructive
(D) construction

2 The gym in the building will be shut down due to the safety ------- taking place on Monday and Tuesday.

(A) inspect
(B) inspector
(C) inspection
(D) inspecting

3 The government agreed to increase ------- rates by 0.8 percent starting next year.

(A) interest
(B) interests
(C) interesting
(D) interested

4 Reading ------- reviews on other websites can help you make a better decision when making a purchase.

(A) produce
(B) production
(C) product
(D) producing

多益實戰詞彙 人物／事物名詞 vs. 抽象名詞

A 請熟記下方可數人物／事物名詞與形態相似的抽象名詞，並分清楚兩者的差異。

an accountant 會計師	accounting 會計（學）
a participant 參與者	participation 參與
a consumer 消費者	consumption 消費
a performer 表演者	a performance 表演
a translator 翻譯師、譯者	(a) translation 翻譯
an employee 員工 an employer 雇主	employment 就業
a founder 創辦人	foundation 創立
an assistant 助理	assistance 協助
a supplier 供應商	(a) supply 供應
a resident 居民	residency 居住
a tenant 租客	(a) tenancy 租賃（期間）
a producer 生產者	production 生產
an investigator 調查人員	(an) investigation 調查
a rival 競爭對手	rivalry 相互較勁
a manager 經理	management 管理
a contributor 捐獻者	(a) contribution 貢獻、捐獻
a supervisor 主管	supervision 監督
a notice 通知、公告	(a) notification 通知

※名詞前如有 (a) 或 (an)，代表該名詞依情況可用作可數名詞或不可數名詞。

B 請選出與中文意思相符的詞彙。

1 就業機會 → (employment / employee) opportunities

2 管理職 → (manager / management) position

3 在某人的監督下 → under the (supervision / supervisor) of someone

4 官方供應商 → official (supplies / supplier)

5 創立年份 → the year of (founder / foundation)

6 租賃期間 → the term of (tenancy / tenant)

7 長期居民 → long-term (residents / residency)

8 徹底的調查 → thorough (investigator / investigation)

9 課堂上的積極參與 → active (participants / participation) in class

10 財務援助 → financial (assistance / assistant)

Practice Test 實戰演練

Part 5 請選出最適合填入空格的字詞。

1. All the visitors to the plant must be aware of the safety ------- at all times.

(A) wearing
(B) regulations
(C) purposes
(D) indication

2. If you would like to strongly express your ------- about the recent changes to the budget, you should be at the meeting.

(A) opinion
(B) distribution
(C) estimate
(D) operation

3. Meat ------- has steadily been increasing since the year 2007.

(A) consume
(B) consumer
(C) consuming
(D) consumption

4. Ms. Kwan's extensive ------- as a manager enabled her to find a better job at an overseas branch.

(A) experience
(B) experienced
(C) experiencing
(D) experiential

5. After years of ------- to her job, Ms. Norman was finally promoted to assistant manager.

(A) experiences
(B) efforts
(C) dedication
(D) experiment

6. Mr. Crooks has been under a lot of ------- since the company is losing money this year.

(A) interests
(B) impression
(C) condition
(D) pressure

7. There are lots of ------- opportunities for educators throughout the country.

(A) employ
(B) employee
(C) employer
(D) employment

8. The company is looking for a competent ------- who can do lots of translation work involving three different languages.

(A) translate
(B) translated
(C) translator
(D) translation

9. The ------- of a local science center is expected to attract more families from cities around the world.

(A) founder
(B) found
(C) founding
(D) foundation

10. If you are looking for a long-term -------, Hilo Gardens Residence is a perfect choice for you.

(A) tenancy
(B) job
(C) landlord
(D) opening

11. I would like to delay the ------- of the copy machine until we can find some space for it.

(A) deliver
(B) delivering
(C) delivery
(D) delivered

12. It came as a great ------- when the agreement was unexpectedly broken.

(A) shock
(B) shocked
(C) shocking
(D) to shock

13. Due to the ------- of shopping malls, more people choose to go to them than to spend time at traditional markets.

(A) convenient
(B) convene
(C) convening
(D) convenience

14. The mobile phone manufacturer is expecting a dramatic increase in sales thanks to the ------- added to the new phone.

(A) featuring
(B) features
(C) featured
(D) to feature

15. The factory ------- is supposed to visit us in order to find out what the problem is.

(A) inspector
(B) inspection
(C) inspect
(D) inspecting

16. Thank you for choosing to spend your holiday with us, and we do hope you have a wonderful time during your -------.

(A) vacate
(B) vacating
(C) vacation
(D) to be vacated

Practice Test

Part 6 請先閱讀文章，再選出適合填入空格的內容。

Questions 17-20 refer to the following memo.

To: All Customer Service Representatives
From: IT Department
Subject: Temporary System Unavailability

This is a ------- (17.) that the IT Department will be replacing some hardware this Friday, January 12, at 12:00 p.m. As such, the main database for our customer information system will be ------- (18.) for approximately 2 hours. However, the Internet will be unaffected, and you will still be able to access your email. Please prepare any data you will need during the temporary shutdown. -------- (19.). We will be sending a ------- (20.) to customers informing them that our services will be limited during this time. If you have any questions, please let us know.

17. (A) remind
(B) reminded
(C) reminding
(D) reminder

18. (A) indicated
(B) unavailable
(C) inconvenient
(D) affordable

19. (A) Don't forget to make copies of any emails you might need.
(B) Do not edit the database.
(C) Please send us the customer information you have on record.
(D) You can download any necessary customer information in advance.

20. (A) notice
(B) notifications
(C) notifying
(D) notices

Part 7 請閱讀文章，並選出正確答案。

Questions 21-22 refer to the following text messages.

Ramesh Adani **[11:04 a.m.]**
Hi, Alex. Sorry to bother you, but I can't access my email account. It says my password is incorrect. Can you help?

Alex Sokolov **[11:06 a.m.]**
Sorry to hear that you're having trouble. I'll reset the password now. Just give me one moment, please.

Ramesh Adani **[11:06 a.m.]**
Sure, take your time.

Alex Sokolov **[11:10 a.m.]**
All right, I've reset your password. You can log in using your employee ID number as the temporary password. Is there anything else I can help with?

Ramesh Adani **[11:11 a.m.]**
Wow, that was fast! Thank you so much. I think that's all I need right now.

Alex Sokolov **[11:12 a.m.]**
I'm glad I could help. Don't forget to change your password after you log in with your temporary password and have a nice day.

21. Why does Mr. Adani message Mr. Sokolov?

(A) To check his employee ID number
(B) To ask for help getting into his email account
(C) To change his login ID
(D) To request a new email address

22. What is probably true about Mr. Sokolov?

(A) He is Mr. Adani's boss.
(B) He is not very familiar with computers.
(C) He works in technical support.
(D) He has a meeting with Mr. Adani later.

Unit 7

代名詞
Pronouns

01 人稱代名詞
02 反身代名詞／指示代名詞
03 不定代名詞

★ 多益實戰詞彙：名詞片語
★ 實戰演練

01 人稱代名詞

STEP 1 題型觀摩

Q Although Ms. Yi has little knowledge of marketing, ------- experience in technical support is extensive.

(A) she
(B) her
(C) hers
(D) herself

Q 雖然李女士對行銷領域不太了解，但她在技術支援方面的資歷卻十分豐富。

(A) 她（人稱代名詞〔主格〕）
(B) 她的（人稱代名詞〔所有格〕）、
她（人稱代名詞〔受格〕）
(C) 她的東西（人稱代名詞〔所有格代名詞〕）
(D) 她自己（反身代名詞）

答案 (B)

命題重點

本題考的是選填適當的人稱代名詞。請先掌握該句話的句型結構，再選出人稱代名詞適當的格。本題空格後面連接名詞 experience（經驗），應填入人稱代名詞的所有格，因此答案為 (B) her。

1 人稱代名詞的單複數、人稱、格的變化

數	人稱	主格	受格	所有格	所有格代名詞
單數	第一人稱（我）	I	me	my	mine
	第二人稱（你）	you	you	your	yours
	第三人稱（他／她／它）	he / she / it	him / her / it	his / her / its	his / hers / -
複數	第一人稱（我們）	we	us	our	ours
	第二人稱（你們）	you	you	your	yours
	第三人稱（他們）	they	them	their	theirs

2 人稱代名詞的主格和受格

主格用來代替名詞，置於主詞的位置；受格則是置於動詞和介系詞的受詞位置。

Mr. Cole will visit the London office, and **he** is scheduled to meet with the president. 〔主詞位置〕
科爾先生將造訪倫敦辦公室，而他已經預定好跟董事長會面。

We interviewed **Jim and Jane** and decided to offer **them** the positions. 〔動詞的受詞位置〕
我們面試過吉姆和珍之後，決定錄用他們。

Please contact **Ms. Park** when you are available to speak to **her**. 〔介系詞的受詞位置〕
等你有時間與朴女士交談時，請再跟她聯絡。

3 所有格和所有格代名詞

所有格會搭配名詞一起使用；所有格代名詞則要單獨置於名詞的位置。

Staff members must use **their** new employee identification cards starting on Monday.
〔所有格＋名詞〕
從週一開始，職員都必須使用自己的新員工證件卡。

Kelly's office is located on the second floor, but **mine** (= my office) is on the third floor. 〔所有格代名詞〕
凱莉的辦公室位於二樓，但我的（＝我的辦公室）位於三樓。

STEP 2 文法練習

請參考句子的中文意思，從提示字詞中選出適當的人稱代名詞填入空格中，並選出該人稱代名詞的種類。

提示	she	mine	your	me	it

1 崔女士在交出離職信前，已經跟經理諮詢過了。
Before Ms. Choi submitted her resignation letter, ______________ consulted with her manager.
（主格 | 受格 | 所有格 | 所有格代名詞）

2 坎培恩先生的職員比我的職員更有經驗。
Mr. Campion's staff is more experienced than ______________.
（主格 | 受格 | 所有格 | 所有格代名詞）

3 請參閱這份報告，因為裡頭包含會議的所有資訊。
Please refer to the report because ______________ has all the information for the meeting.
（主格 | 受格 | 所有格 | 所有格代名詞）

4 我們可能無法在週末幫您安排到您平常看診的醫生。
On the weekend, you might not be scheduled to see ______________ usual doctor.
（主格 | 受格 | 所有格 | 所有格代名詞）

5 我的直屬主管今天早上因為我上班遲到而打電話給我。
My immediate supervisor called ______________ this morning because I was late to work.
（主格 | 受格 | 所有格 | 所有格代名詞）

STEP 3 試題演練

請選出最適合填入空格的字詞。

1 Employees who get an A on ------- performance review will be likely to get promotions.

(A) they
(B) them
(C) their
(D) theirs

2 City officials have announced that ------- will close 11th Avenue for repairs until April 4.

(A) they
(B) them
(C) their
(D) theirs

3 Ms. Smith's promotion means that ------- has to transfer to headquarters.

(A) she
(B) her
(C) hers
(D) herself

4 When picking up a passport, you need to show ------- another form of identification.

(A) we
(B) us
(C) our
(D) ourselves

02 反身代名詞／指示代名詞

STEP 1 題型觀摩

Q The participants discussed the issues among ------- after the seminar ended.
(A) they
(B) them
(C) their
(D) themselves

Q 研討會結束後，學員即自行討論相關議題。
(A) 他們（人稱代名詞〔主格〕）
(B) 他們（人稱代名詞〔受格〕）
(C) 他們的（人稱代名詞〔所有格〕）
(D) 他們自己（反身代名詞）

答案 (D)

人稱代名詞考題中，當空格置於介系詞後方時，答案須選擇人稱代名詞的受格，或是反身代名詞。根據本題題意，空格指的是跟主詞相同的一群人，因此答案要選反身代名詞 (D) themselves。

1 反身代名詞置於受詞的位置

反身代名詞表示「……自己」的意思。**當主詞和受詞相同時，受詞的位置會使用反身代名詞**，不使用人稱代名詞的受格。

	第一人稱	第二人稱	第三人稱
單數	myself 我自己	yourself 你自己	himself 他自己 herself 她自己 itself 它自己
複數	ourselves 我們自己	yourselves 你們自己	themselves 他／她／它們自己

Mr. Taylor blamed <u>himself</u> for the accident. 〔Mr. Taylor = himself〕
泰勒先生責備自己造成這場意外。

Mr. Taylor blamed <u>him</u> for the accident. 〔Mr. Taylor ≠ him〕
泰勒先生責備他造成這場意外。〔「他」＝泰勒先生以外的人〕

2 用反身代名詞來強調主詞

用於強調主詞的反身代名詞，意思為「**親自、親手**」。此時，**即使省略反身代名詞，也不會影響句子的完整性**。

The sales manager emphasized that he <u>himself</u> wrote the report.
業務經理強調報告是他自己寫的。

具代表性的反身代名詞用法
by oneself 獨自（做）……、自己（做）……
for oneself 獨自（做）……、為自己（做）……
of itself 本身、本質上

3 指示代名詞 this / these / that / those

指示代名詞用來代替**前面提過的名詞**。另外，「**those who . . .**」有「**……的人**」的意思。

The figures in the report are better than <u>those</u> of the previous one. 〔those = figures〕
報告裡的數字比上一份報告的數字好。

<u>Those who</u> cannot attend the meeting should let me know in advance. 〔those =人們〕
無法來開會的人應該事先通知我。

STEP 2 文法練習

請參考句子的中文意思，從提示字詞中選出適當的代名詞填入空格中。

提示	those	himself	herself	that	yourself

1 具備四年工作資歷的人可應徵此職位。
______________ with 4 years of job experience can apply for this position.

2 新款智慧型手機的價格比舊款價格更貴。
The price of the new smartphone is more expensive than ______________ of the old one.

3 你必須獨自籌備盛大開幕活動。
You have to organize the grand opening events by ______________.

4 盧女士讓自己在加班過後休息一下。
Ms. Lu gave ______________ a break from working overtime.

5 派特森先生強調他本人會對最終決策負起責任。
Mr. Paterson emphasized he ______________ would be responsible for the final decision.

STEP 3 試題演練

請選出最適合填入空格的字詞。

1 ------- who are interested in the IT training course should talk to Ms. Kelly in Human Resources.

(A) That
(B) Those
(C) Anyone
(D) Them

2 Please prepare ------- for inclement weather conditions when you get to your final destination.

(A) you
(B) your
(C) yours
(D) yourself

3 Ms. Munroe is scheduled to visit London and will finalize the agreement with the client on ------- own.

(A) she
(B) her
(C) its
(D) herself

4 According to market research, Dyco's latest vacuum cleaner is quite similar to ------- of LK Electronics.

(A) that
(B) those
(C) this
(D) it

03 不定代名詞

STEP 1 題型觀摩

Q Ms. Gupta announced that she will replace the seats and sound systems in ------- of her theaters.

(A) all
(B) any
(C) little
(D) much

Q 古普塔女士宣布，她將更換旗下所有電影院的座椅和音響系統。

(A) 所有
(B) 任何
(C) 很少
(D) 許多

答案 (A)

請務必熟記「不定代名詞＋ of the ＋複數可數名詞」的用法。四個選項中，any 一般用於否定句或疑問句、little 和 much 要搭配不可數名詞一起使用，因此皆不適合作為答案。綜合前述內容，答案為 (A) all，可搭配複數可數名詞一起使用。

1 以不定代名詞表示全體中的一部分

不定代名詞＋ of the／所有格＋不可數名詞＋單數動詞

some of the information **is** 部分資訊是……	**any** of the information **is** 任何資訊是……
all of the information **is** 所有資訊是……	**most** of the information **is** 大部分資訊是……
much of the information **is** 許多資訊是……	**a little / little** of the information **is** 一些／幾乎沒有資訊是……

不定代名詞＋ of the／所有格＋可數名詞複數＋複數動詞

some of the products **are** 部分產品是……	**any** of the products **are** 任何產品是……
all of the products **are** 所有產品是……	**most** of the products **are** 大部分產品是……
many of the products **are** 許多產品是……	**a few / few** of the products **are** 一些／幾乎沒有產品是……

each of the products **is** 每項產品是……〔連接可數名詞複數，但動詞為單數〕
none of the products **is/are** 沒有產品是……〔連接可數名詞複數，動詞單複數皆可〕

※every（每一個）只能當形容詞，不能當代名詞，因此沒有「every of the . . .」的用法（every 的用法請見 p. 98）。

2 one / another / the other(s) / others / each other / one another

one 一個
another 另一個（泛指「三者以上不特定的一個」）
the other 另一個（特指「兩者當中剩下的那一個」）
others 其他人事物（泛指「不特定多數」）
the others 其他人事物（特指「一組當中剩下的」）
each other（兩者）彼此
one another（三者以上）彼此

3 表示兩者之一、兩者皆是、兩者皆非的不定代名詞

either of the products **is** 兩項產品之中的某一項會……〔連接可數名詞複數，但動詞為單數〕
both of the products **are** 兩項產品都會……
neither of the products **is/are** 兩項產品都不會……〔連接可數名詞複數，動詞單複數皆可〕

STEP 2 文法練習

請參考句子的中文意思，從提示字詞中選出適當的代名詞填入空格中。

提示	another	most	each other	some	all

1 金先生和崔女士在開會時彼此交談。
Mr. Kim and Ms. Choi talked to ______________ during the meeting.

2 有些員工的評價很好，有些則差強人意。
______________ of the employees got great reviews, but some did not.

3 門羅先生在上海開設了他第一家工廠，並已經決定再開一家。
Mr. Munroe opened his first factory in Shanghai, and he has decided to open ______________.

4 大部分與會者都無法參加會議後的派對。
______________ of the participants cannot attend the party after the conference.

5 蘭妮絲特女士建議審閱文件裡的所有資料。
Ms. Lannister suggested reviewing ______________ of the information in the documents.

STEP 3 試題演練

請選出最適合填入空格的字詞。

1 Mr. Garcia stated in the letter of recommendation that Ms. Ling works very well with --------.
(A) other
(B) another
(C) others
(D) both

2 Mr. Patel is not here today, but he has not missed ------- of the board meetings this year.
(A) any
(B) some
(C) a little
(D) either

3 Concord Electronics' Gala smartphone is currently the lightest ------- on the market.
(A) another
(B) one
(C) any
(D) either

4 Ms. Rufus could not answer ------- of the two questions she received at the technology seminar.
(A) both
(B) either
(C) neither
(D) every

多益實戰詞彙 名詞片語

A 請熟記下方高頻率名詞片語。

quality control 品質管理	job performance 工作表現
reliable service 可靠的服務	performance review 績效考核
company policy 公司政策	night shift（輪值）夜班
safety procedure 安全程序	feasible plan 可行的計畫
seating capacity 可容納的座位數量	customized service 客製化服務
advance registration 事先報名	bulky item 大型物品
competitive market 競爭市場	valid ticket 有效票券
competitive edge 競爭優勢	sales quota 業績配額（業務人員在一定的時間內須達成的銷售量）
competent candidate 適任的應徵者／候選人	preliminary survey 初步調查
competent leader 適任的領導人	slight flaw 輕微瑕疵
further notice 進一步的通知	defective item 瑕疵品
incentive plans 獎勵計畫	proof of purchase 購買證明
tax incentives 租稅誘因（政府透過減稅，以鼓勵企業或個人的經濟活動）	expiration date 到期日
sales figures 銷售數據	customs official 海關官員
leading figure 領導人物	baggage allowance 行李限額
overhead expenses 營運費用	method of payment 付款方法
outstanding expenses 未付費用	luxury commodity 奢侈品
economic stability 經濟穩定	home appliance 家用電器

B 請選出與中文意思相符的詞彙。

1 進行績效考核 → conduct performance (reviews / restore)

2 初步調查結果 → the results of the preliminary (survey / installation)

3 審閱銷售數據 → review sales (features / figures)

4 遵從安全程序 → follow safety (processes / procedures)

5 對奢侈品課以重稅 → pose high taxes on luxury (commodities / equipment)

6 想出一個可行的計畫 → come up with a feasible (plan / consent)

7 最為適任的應徵者 → the most competent (candidate / application)

8 需要更好的品質管理 → need better (quantity / quality) control

9 追求經濟穩定 → pursue economic (capacity / stability)

10 需要事先報名 → require advance (registration / revision)

Practice Test 實戰演練

Part 5 請選出最適合填入空格的字詞。

1. The vice president of KTS Finance rides ------- bike to work every morning to avoid traffic.

   (A) he
   (B) him
   (C) his
   (D) himself

2. Mr. Carpenter kept 100 dollars for ------- and gave away most of his money to charity.

   (A) he
   (B) him
   (C) his
   (D) himself

3. Since the entire staff was busy, Ms. Garcia had to work overtime to complete the project by -------.

   (A) she
   (B) her
   (C) hers
   (D) herself

4. Employees at Stanley Bank will receive additional pay when ------- work on Saturday or Sunday.

   (A) they
   (B) them
   (C) their
   (D) themselves

5. No one expected Mr. Oliver to handle the difficulties ------- without asking for any assistance.

   (A) he
   (B) him
   (C) his
   (D) himself

6. Many employees at the meeting have industrial experience, but only some of ------- can understand the presentation.

   (A) we
   (B) us
   (C) our
   (D) ourselves

7. Ms. Liu and Ms. Wang started working for the Ecolin Corporation at the same time, and ------- of them got promoted this month.

   (A) both
   (B) every
   (C) many
   (D) much

8. High-rise buildings cannot be built in areas where they can block the views of -------.

   (A) ones
   (B) others
   (C) another
   (D) themselves

9. The new bookstore is crowded with customers, but ------- will not make any purchases.

(A) every
(B) little
(C) some
(D) one

10. Pease take a look at ------- website for further information regarding our latest equipment.

(A) we
(B) us
(C) our
(D) ours

11. Most of the employees have been working overtime to meet their sales ------- for the first quarter.

(A) proximity
(B) quota
(C) basis
(D) reputation

12. The companies in the shipping industry need to develop a competitive ------- to win contracts.

(A) edge
(B) shift
(C) claim
(D) demand

13. Ms. Chun wanted to know when the first draft of the contract would be ready for ------- to review.

(A) she
(B) her
(C) hers
(D) herself

14. All of the baggage at the airport in New York will be thoroughly checked by ------- officials.

(A) customs
(B) customers
(C) competence
(D) comparable

15. ------- of the proposals to build cultural and sports facilities in the city are likely to be approved this week.

(A) Little
(B) All
(C) Every
(D) Any

16. The city government is trying to adopt a new ------- of payment for small businesses.

(A) capacity
(B) material
(C) role
(D) method

Part 6 請先閱讀文章，再選出適合填入空格的內容。

Questions 17-20 refer to the following email.

To: mia.a@ymail.com
From: m_issa@zod.com
Date: January 19
Subject: Update about recent order

Dear Mrs. Alexopoulos,

Thank you for your recent order from ------- **17.** website. We hope that you were able to find everything you needed.

I regret to inform you, however, that the solid oak work desk (part #33454) ------- **18.** ordered is currently sold out. The rest of your order will be shipped immediately, but this item will be delayed until we receive more items from our factory. -------. **19.** I'm very sorry for any inconvenience this causes you.

Thank you for understanding, and I apologize again for the trouble. If you have any questions, don't ------- **20.** to contact us.

Sincerely,

Mohamed Issa
Zenith Office Direct

17. (A) we
(B) us
(C) our
(D) ours

18. (A) you
(B) your
(C) yours
(D) yourself

19. (A) I will let you know as soon as it ships.
(B) There should be no problem completing your refund.
(C) Our website will be unavailable until Sunday.
(D) You will receive an invoice by the end of the day.

20. (A) hesitate
(B) hesitant
(C) hesitating
(D) hesitation

Part 7 請閱讀文章，並選出正確答案。

Questions 21-23 refer to the following invoice.

Prime Depot
44 Brown Street
London
W1T 1JY

Date	June 22	**Invoice Number**	901AK
Bill to	JR Law Firm, 83 Mare Street, London, SW1A		

Item	Price/Unit	Total
6 x A4 Paper Crate	$80.00	$480.00
12 x Red Ballpoint Pen (Box)	$6.50	$78.00
4 x Copy Toner Refill	$25.00	$100.00
6 x Standard Envelope (Box)	$8.00	$48.00
6 x Document Envelope (Box)	$12.00	$72.00
	Subtotal	$778.00
	Tax	$69.24
	Total	$847.24

Payment may be made in cash or by check on delivery or by credit card in advance.

21. What most likely is Prime Depot?

(A) A finance office
(B) A law firm
(C) An office supply company
(D) A printing company

22. How many boxes of A4 paper did the JR Law Firm order?

(A) 4
(B) 6
(C) 8
(D) 12

23. What is mentioned as a possible payment option?

(A) Card prepayment
(B) Bank transfer
(C) Cash in advance
(D) Gift cards in person

Unit 8

形容詞
Adjectives

01 形容詞的角色

02 數量形容詞

03 須注意的形容詞搭配組合

★ 多益實戰詞彙：易混淆形容詞

★ 實戰演練

Unit 8

01 形容詞的角色

STEP 1 題型觀摩

Q The number of people with ------- income is increasing more and more. (A) dispose (B) disposable (C) disposability (D) disposition	**Q** 擁有可支配所得的人數越來越多。 (A) 處置（原形動詞、現在簡單式） (B) 可支配的（形容詞） (C) 一次性（名詞） (D) 傾向（名詞） ※「disposable income」（可支配所得）指「所得總額減掉稅金等無法自由支配使用之非消費支出，剩下的可自由支配的那一部分所得」。 答案 (B)

命題重點 空格後面出現名詞 income（收入），表示應選擇形容詞作為答案。形容詞 disposable（可支配的）放在名詞前面作修飾，故答案為 (B)。

1 置於名詞前面作修飾

將形容詞置於名詞前面，扮演**修飾名詞**的角色。

A thorough investigation will be done wherever necessary. 〔冠詞＋形容詞＋名詞〕
（我們）會在必要的地方進行徹底的調查。

You are required to make **a very careful decision** this time. 〔冠詞＋副詞＋形容詞＋名詞〕
你這次必須做出十分謹慎的決定。

2 說明主詞的狀態（扮演主詞補語的角色）

將形容詞置於 be（是……）、become（變成……）等動詞後面，**補充說明主詞的狀態**。

連接形容詞當作主詞補語的動詞		
remain 維持……的狀態	stay 保持……的狀態	turn 變成……
seem 似乎……	appear 似乎……、看起來像是……	

The company **is** not **ready** for the launch of the new product. 〔be 動詞＋形容詞〕
公司尚未做好新品上市的準備。

3 說明受詞的狀態（扮演受詞補語的角色）

將形容詞置於受詞後面，**補充說明受詞的狀態**。

連接形容詞當作受詞補語的動詞		
keep 讓……保持……的狀態	leave 放任……保持……的狀態	consider 認為……是……
make 使……變成……	find 覺得……是……	

This new software will **keep** your office computers **safe**. 〔動詞 keep ＋受詞＋形容詞〕
這個新軟體能讓您公司的電腦保持在安全狀態之下。

STEP 2 文法練習

請參考句子的中文意思，從提示字詞中選出適當的形容詞填入空格中，並選出該形容詞所扮演的角色。

提示	informed	silent	healthy	calm	open

1 發生緊急狀況時請保持冷靜。
Please try to stay ______________ when there is an emergency.
（修飾名詞 | 主詞補語 | 受詞補語）

2 可以請你出門時讓窗戶保持開著嗎？
Would you please leave the windows ______________ when you go out?
（修飾名詞 | 主詞補語 | 受詞補語）

3 董事長在簡報過程中一直保持沉默。
The president remained ______________ during the presentation.
（修飾名詞 | 主詞補語 | 受詞補語）

4 每天服用綜合維他命能讓你保持身體健康。
Taking multivitamins every day will keep you ______________.
（修飾名詞 | 主詞補語 | 受詞補語）

5 我們會持續為您更新這項產品的最新消息。
We will keep you ______________ on the latest updates on this product.
（修飾名詞 | 主詞補語 | 受詞補語）

STEP 3 試題演練

請選出最適合填入空格的字詞。

1 Mr. Wilson is always welcome to accept ------- ideas from his team members.
(A) create
(B) creative
(C) creation
(D) creatively

2 You will find the attached manual ------- when you are trying to assemble the device.
(A) use
(B) using
(C) useful
(D) usefully

3 Please be ------- of others when you are staying in the library.
(A) consider
(B) considerate
(C) consideration
(D) considering

4 We are willing to take every ------- action in order to avoid the kinds of problems that we had last year.
(A) possible
(B) possibly
(C) possibility
(D) be possible

02 數量形容詞

STEP 1 題型觀摩

Q ------- participant is going to have to present a valid ID in order to enter the venue.

(A) All
(B) Some
(C) Every
(D) A majority of

Q 每一位參與者進入場館時，都必須出示有效的身分證件。

(A) 所有（數量形容詞〔可數名詞複數／不可數名詞〕）
(B) 部分（數量形容詞〔可數名詞複數／不可數名詞〕）
(C) 每一個（數量形容詞〔可數名詞單數〕）
(D) 大多數（數量形容詞〔可數名詞複數〕）

答案 (C)

命題重點 這類題型要選出適合搭配後面名詞使用的數量形容詞。空格後面的名詞 participant（參與者）為單數，適合與其搭配使用的數量形容詞為 every（每一個），故正確答案為 (C)。

數量形容詞的種類

數量形容詞搭配的名詞，取決於該名詞所表示的數量，因此請留意數量形容詞後面連接的名詞，選出適當的搭配。

數量形容詞	搭配的名詞
all 全部 some 部分、一些 any 任何 most 大部分 no 沒有…… lots of / a lot of / plenty of 很多	＋可數名詞複數或不可數名詞 例 some trainees 部分學員 some advice 一些建議 most problems 大部分問題 most of the time 大部分時間 lots of people 很多人 lots of time 很多時間
every 每一個 each 每一個 another 另一個	＋可數名詞單數 例 each participant 每位參與者 every effort 每一份努力 another issue 另一個議題 ※each 可以當代名詞單獨使用（如「each of the . . .」，請見 p. 88），但 every 只能當形容詞，後面一定要接上名詞。
many 許多 a number of 眾多 a majority of 大多數 a variety of 各式各樣 several 幾個、若干 a couple of 若干、兩三個 a few 一些 few 幾乎沒有	＋可數名詞複數 例 a number of complaints 眾多抱怨 a majority of applicants 大多數的應徵者 a couple of questions 若干問題
a great deal of / much 大量、許多 a little 一些 little 幾乎沒有	＋不可數名詞 例 a great deal of research 大量的研究 a little time left 剩一些時間

Every sales representative should attend the seminar without **any** exceptions.
每一名業務代表都必須參加研討會，沒有任何例外。

STEP 2 文法練習

請參考句子的中文意思，從提示字詞中選出適當的數量形容詞填入空格中。

提示	some	much	all	no	each	every

1 我們認為準備工作結束後不會剩很多時間。
We expect there won't be ______________ time left for the preparation.

2 所有的參與者都應該配戴名牌。
______________ participants are required to wear a name tag.

3 這裡的大部分工人都不在乎安全問題。
Most of the workers here have ______________ concern for safety.

4 你得非常謹慎地閱讀每一條指示才行。
You should read ______________ of the directions very carefully.

5 我們在仔細檢查報告的時候，發現了一些不合理之處。
While we were going over the report, we found ______________ irregularities.

STEP 3 試題演練

請選出最適合填入空格的字詞。

1 Office Works offers a ------- of office supplies and furniture.
(A) varying
(B) varied
(C) variable
(D) variety

2 ------- employee is required to obtain permission from a manager before taking a day off.
(A) Both
(B) Either
(C) Every
(D) Some

3 We had consulted ------- focus groups before we finished this report.
(A) a couple of
(B) a little
(C) any
(D) a great deal of

4 A recent survey revealed that some customers don't have ------- trust in our products.
(A) many
(B) much
(C) a couple of
(D) few

03 須注意的形容詞搭配組合

STEP 1 題型觀摩

Q Nobody is capable ------- doing the job so successfully.

(A) with

(B) to

(C) of

(D) from

Q 沒有人能如此成功地完成這項任務。

(A) with

(B) to

(C) of

(D) from

答案 (C)

該類考題考的是搭配特定形容詞使用的介系詞，或是搭配特定介系詞使用的形容詞。「be capable of」的意思為「有能力做……」，故答案應選 (C) of。請熟記常考的形容詞搭配組合。

1 「be ＋形容詞＋不定詞 to V」的組合

be able to 有能力做……	be willing to 願意做……
be likely to 很有可能會做……	be ready to 準備好要做……
be sure/bound/certain to 絕對會做……	be hesitant to 猶豫要不要做……
be eligible to 有資格做……	be happy/pleased/delighted to 樂意做……、愉快地做……
be eager to 急切想做……	be/feel free to 自在地做……、不吝做……

Customers will **be willing to** pay more money as long as better quality is guaranteed.
只要能保證品質更好，顧客就會願意付更多的錢。

2 「be ＋形容詞＋介系詞」的組合

be capable of 有能力做……	be responsible for 對……負責、負責……
be aware of 意識到……	be suitable for 適合……
be critical of 對……批判	be similar to 與……相似
be familiar with 熟悉……	be relevant to 與……有關
be consistent with 與……一致	be subject to 容易……、有……的傾向
be compatible with 與……相容	be equivalent to 與……同等
be happy with 對……感到開心／滿意	be accessible to 可進入／接近／使用……
be eligible for 有權獲得……、有權使用……	be absent from 未出現於……
be famous for 因為……而知名	be different from 與……不同

This training schedule **is subject to** change.
這項教育訓練的時程可能會隨時調整。

Childcare specialists suggest that parents **be consistent with** their discipline methods.
育兒專家建議家長的教養方法須有一致性。

STEP 2 文法練習

請參考句子的中文意思，從提示字詞中選出適當的形容詞搭配組合填入空格中。

提示			
	capable of	eligible to	familiar with
	able to	aware of	accessible to

1 所有與會者都有資格參加抽獎。
All participants are ______________ enter the lucky draw.

2 我們無法確定問題的成因。
We were not ______________ identify what the cause of the problem was.

3 請注意這項產品的潛在危險性。
Please be ______________ the potential dangers of this product.

4 在這棟大樓工作的任何人都可以利用附設的圖書館。
The in-house library is ______________ anybody working in this building.

5 可惜新任經理對財務計畫不甚熟悉。
Unfortunately, the new manager was not ______________ the financial program.

STEP 3 試題演練

請選出最適合填入空格的字詞。

1 Please note that this program schedule is ------- to change without notice.
(A) able
(B) subject
(C) equivalent
(D) consistent

2 The company is not ------- for any goods or services you obtain.
(A) ready
(B) responsible
(C) aware
(D) comparable

3 The Atlantic Steakhouse is planning to invite all the reviewers who were ------- of its new menu.
(A) critical
(B) critic
(C) critics
(D) criticism

4 A team of marketing specialists will determine whether the new strategy is ------- for the promotion of our products.
(A) famous
(B) applicable
(C) suitable
(D) likely

多益實戰詞彙 易混淆形容詞

A 下面列出形態相似、意思不同的形容詞，請比較兩者的差異後，熟記各自對應的中文意思。

apprehensive 擔心的	apprehensible 可理解的
beneficial 有益的	beneficent 仁慈的
comparable 與……相當的、與……並駕齊驅的	compatible 相容的
considerate 體貼的、替人著想的	considerable 大量的
complimentary 免費的	complementary 補充的
confident 有自信的	confidential 機密的
dependent 對……依賴的	dependable 可靠的
favorable 有利的	favorite 最喜歡的
last 最後的	lasting 持久的
manageable 有辦法處理的	managerial 管理的
prospective 潛在的	prosperous 繁榮的
personal 個人的	personnel 人事的
preventive 預防性的	preventable 可避免的
reliant 依賴的	reliable 可靠的
responsible 有責任感的、對……有責任的	responsive 反應積極的
successful 成功的	successive 連續的
understanding 善解人意的	understandable 可理解的

B 請選出與中文意思相符的詞彙。

1 預防性措施 → (preventive / preventable) measures

2 機密文件 → (confidential / confident) documents

3 管理職 → (manageable / managerial) position

4 潛在學生、未來的學生 → (prosperous / prospective) students

5 連續的失敗 → (successful / successive) failure

6 對顧客需求反應積極 → (responsive / responsible) to customer needs

7 持久的結果 → (long-lasting / long-last) results

8 與新設備相容 → (compatible / comparable) with new devices

9 對雙方都有益 → (beneficent / beneficial) to mutual parties

10 可靠的供應商 → (dependent / dependable) suppliers

Practice Test 實戰演練

Part 5 請選出最適合填入空格的字詞。

1. Feel free to contact any of our representatives if you have ------- inquiries.
   (A) either
   (B) any
   (C) none
   (D) few

2. It is important that all the documents that we deal with here be kept -------.
   (A) confidential
   (B) confidence
   (C) confidentially
   (D) confident

3. The Labor Review Board recently published a ------- research study on the effects of a 20-minute break on the efficiency of factory workers.
   (A) comprehend
   (B) comprehensive
   (C) comprehensively
   (D) comprehending

4. If you want to purchase modern furniture items at ------- prices, please visit one of our offline stores.
   (A) afford
   (B) afforded
   (C) affordable
   (D) affording

5. They created a company 20 years ago to provide a ------- vacation experience.
   (A) special
   (B) specially
   (C) specialty
   (D) specific

6. The only ------- conference room is on the ground floor of the building.
   (A) available
   (B) previous
   (C) advanced
   (D) personal

7. A new government policy will be implemented to make health insurance ------- to more people.
   (A) accessible
   (B) considerable
   (C) apprehensible
   (D) diverse

8. After the website is upgraded, customers will be able to enjoy a(n) ------- advantage while they shop online.
   (A) applicable
   (B) experienced
   (C) distinct
   (D) different

9. As a ------- measure, you should back up your files when you work on the computer.

(A) successive
(B) preventive
(C) projective
(D) complementary

10. It usually takes more than 10 years to get in a ------- position after graduation.

(A) manageable
(B) prosperous
(C) versatile
(D) managerial

11. Please do not keep your ------- belongings unattended when you leave your seat.

(A) personal
(B) promising
(C) personnel
(D) prospective

12. Although two candidates have different academic backgrounds, they are ------- in terms of their work experience.

(A) reasonable
(B) comparable
(C) available
(D) responsive

13. We are pleased to provide you with a ------- salad bar with lots of vegetables and fruits.

(A) compatible
(B) subsequent
(C) complimentary
(D) indifferent

14. If your customers' responses are not -------, you may want to change your way of doing business.

(A) favorite
(B) favorable
(C) considerate
(D) comparable

15. Please be ------- of other visitors when you talk on the phone in public.

(A) considerable
(B) considerate
(C) considering
(D) conclusive

16. If you have any questions about benefits for employees, you should contact the ------- department.

(A) dependent
(B) competitive
(C) countable
(D) personnel

Part 6 請先閱讀文章，再選出適合填入空格的內容。

Questions 17-20 refer to the following letter.

Dear Ms. Taylor,

Thank you for your letter dated June 22. I am so sorry to hear that you were not -------(**17.**) with the service we provided during your trip to the city last week. First of all, I -------(**18.**) apologize that your room was not properly cleaned when you arrived. I understand how unpleasant that felt. -------(**19.**) With regard to the room service, I am sorry that your breakfast arrived so late that you had to leave without eating. This is totally -------(**20.**), and I will make sure something like this doesn't happen again.

Sincerely,
Albert Williams

17. (A) consistent
(B) happy
(C) suitable
(D) valuable

18. (A) carefully
(B) sincerely
(C) skillfully
(D) unexpectedly

19. (A) I hope you have a pleasant stay.
(B) We are not responsible for any of the damage.
(C) I will speak to the cleaning services manager right away.
(D) We don't provide complimentary breakfast service anymore.

20. (A) famous
(B) applicable
(C) unsuitable
(D) likely

Part 7 請閱讀文章，並選出正確答案。

Questions 21-22 refer to the following email.

From:	hr@globaltech.com
To:	lmartinez@jmail.com
Subject:	RE: Application Questions

Dear Ms. Martinez,

Thank you for your inquiry about the senior marketing coordinator position here at Global Tech. I apologize for the late reply. To answer your questions about the application process, all applicants must first submit an online application no later than September 17. You can find the online form on our company's Career page. Please note that you will need the following information in order to complete the application:

- a résumé & description of your work history
- a cover letter
- copies of all relevant certifications and licenses
- copies of any diplomas you have

Your completed application packet will be received by the hiring committee, who will then make the final decision about who will move on to the interview stage. If selected for an interview, we will contact you by email to schedule a time. If you have any other questions or would like additional information, please don't hesitate to contact us. I look forward to speaking with you soon.

Sincerely,
Dorothy Hamill
HR Representative
Global Tech, Inc.

21. What did Ms. Martinez most likely inquire about in her email?

(A) A position's responsibilities
(B) The qualifications required for a position
(C) The process of applying for a position
(D) Some contact information

22. Which of the following is NOT required to submit an application?

(A) Contact information for references
(B) A résumé and a cover letter
(C) A certificate of graduation
(D) An online application

Unit 9

副詞
Adverbs

01 副詞的角色和位置

STEP 1 題型觀摩

Q Ms. Watson has been recognized as an ------- talented singer and composer.	Q 華森女士一直被認為是一位特別有才華的歌手與作曲家。
(A) exceptional	(A) 特別的（形容詞）
(B) exception	(B) 特例（名詞）
(C) exceptionally	(C) 特別地（副詞）
(D) excepted	(D) 除了……之外的（形容詞，只能放名詞後）
	答案 (C)

命題重點 掌握題目的句型結構後，便能判斷出適合填入空格的詞性。在本題中，句型結構為「冠詞＋（空格）＋形容詞＋名詞」，**空格內應填入副詞，用來修飾後面的形容詞**，因此答案為副詞 (C) exceptionally，意思為「特別地」。

副詞可以用來修飾整個句子，或是動詞／形容詞／副詞等

副詞扮演進一步說明句子意思的角色，因此**即使句子省略副詞，也不會影響其完整性**。副詞的種類和意思繁多，可置於句中不同的位置。

(1) 修飾**整個句子**／修飾**動詞**（置於主詞和動詞之間）

修飾整個句子		He hasn't seen her **lately**.〔置於句末〕他最近都沒見到她。 **Recently**, she was promoted.〔置於句首〕她最近剛升職。
修飾動詞	副詞＋動詞	Ms. Yang **suddenly*** **quit** her job. 楊女士突然辭職了。 *副詞不能置於及物動詞和受詞之間 (quit suddenly her job [X])。
	助動詞＋副詞＋主要動詞	It can **seriously affect** the company. 這個情況會嚴重影響公司。
	have ＋副詞＋ p.p.	Mr. Lim has **positively influenced** him. 林先生對他產生正面的影響。
	be ＋副詞＋ p.p.	The man was **badly injured**. 這個人受了重傷。
	be ＋副詞＋ V-ing	We are **seriously considering** it. 我們正在認真考慮這件事。

(2) 修飾**形容詞**、**副詞**、**不定詞**、**動名詞**

修飾形容詞	That is a **surprisingly good** result.〔冠詞＋副詞＋形容詞＋名詞〕 這真的是令人驚訝的好結果。
修飾副詞	Ms. Song performed **very well**.〔副詞＋副詞〕 宋女士表演得非常好。
修飾不定詞	I am glad **to finally meet** you, Mr. Kang. 姜先生，我很高興終於見到您。
修飾動名詞	By **carefully reviewing** the survey results, they improved its design. 藉由謹慎審閱問卷的結果，他們得以改善這項產品的設計。

STEP 2 文法練習

請參考句子的中文意思，從提示字詞中選出適當的副詞填入空格中，並選出該副詞所扮演的角色。

提示	very	finally	relatively	surprisingly	patiently

1 要有耐心等到換你發言，這是很重要的能力。
It is important to ________ wait for your turn to speak.
（修飾副詞 | 修飾動名詞 | 修飾不定詞 to V）

2 令人驚訝的是，顧客問卷調查的結果十分樂觀。
________, the results of the customer survey were positive.
（修飾形容詞 | 修飾動詞 | 修飾整個句子）

3 阿靈頓先生將 20 名職員管理得非常好。
Mr. Arlington supervised a staff of twenty people ________ well.
（修飾動名詞 | 修飾形容詞 | 修飾副詞）

4 新的體育場館終於要在下週二開幕了。
The new sports complex is ________ opening next Tuesday.
（修飾動詞 | 修飾不定詞 to V | 修飾副詞）

5 他們針對這個問題，擬定出相對簡易的解決方案。
They developed a ________ simple solution to the problem.
（修飾整個句子 | 修飾副詞 | 修飾形容詞）

STEP 3 試題演練

請選出最適合填入空格的字詞。

1 The head of Marketing believes that Mr. Casey can ------- manage the new advertising campaign.
(A) success
(B) succession
(C) successful
(D) successfully

2 The engineers can restore and display a list of ------- opened files and folders if necessary.
(A) recent
(B) recency
(C) recently
(D) recentness

3 Mr. Smith, who has been with the company for 30 years, is ------- considering resigning at the end of the year.
(A) serious
(B) seriously
(C) seriousness
(D) being serious

4 -------, the board of directors has decided to close down the factories located in East Asian countries.
(A) Unfortunate
(B) Unfortunately
(C) Unfortunates
(D) Unfortunateness

02 頻率／時間／連接副詞

STEP 1 題型觀摩

Q It is only the first quarter, and the KI Corporation has ------- had to close the factory twice because of strikes. (A) already (B) further (C) most (D) carefully	**Q** 目前才第一季而已，KI 企業卻已經因為罷工事件而必須閉廠兩次。 (A) 已經 (B) 進一步 (C) 大部分 (D) 仔細地 答案 (A)

該句話表達的內容為「公司才第一季就歷經兩次閉廠」，因此空格填入 (A) already（已經）較為適當，指「某事件發生的時間比預期的早」。

1 頻率副詞

頻率副詞表示事情發生的頻率，置於 be 動詞後面或一般動詞前面。

100%				50%		0%
always 總是	usually/normally 通常	often 常常	sometimes 有時候	occasionally 偶爾	seldom/hardly/rarely 很少、幾乎沒有	never 從未

The shop **is** **normally** crowded between 2 p.m. and 4 p.m. 〔置於 be 動詞後面〕
這間商店通常在下午 2 點到 4 點之間人潮擁擠。

Some of the employees **always** **go** for a walk after lunch. 〔置於一般動詞前面〕
有些員工總是在午餐之後散步。

2 時間副詞

already 已經	soon 很快、馬上	still 仍然	just 剛才	yet 尚未

She has **already** completed the budget report.
她已經完成預算報告了。

Mr. Lee hasn't applied for a job **yet***.
李先生尚未應徵工作。

*yet 也有「have yet to V」的用法，沒有 not，但有否定的意義，如：I have yet to read the book.（我還沒讀這本書。）。

3 連接副詞

表轉折	however 然而　nevertheless/nonetheless 然而、儘管如此
表因果關係	therefore 因此　consequently 所以
表附加概念	moreover/furthermore 此外　besides 況且、還有

Jim resigned last month. **However**, no one has been hired to fill his position. 〔連接副詞的位置〕
吉姆上個月辭職了。然而，公司尚未僱用別人來填補他的職缺。

Jim resigned last month, **but** no one has been hired to fill his position. 〔連接詞的位置應使用 but〕
→ however [X]
吉姆上個月辭職了，但是公司尚未僱用別人來填補他的職缺。

STEP 2 文法練習

請參考句子的中文意思，從提示字詞中選出適當的副詞填入空格中。

提示	rarely	sometimes	moreover	still	already

1 公司有時候會在下班後舉辦員工聚餐。
The company ________ holds staff dinners after work.

2 員工很少在公司大樓裡抽菸。
Employees ________ smoke in the company building.

3 團隊成員仍有很多工作需要完成。
The team members ________ have a lot of work to finish.

4 金先生已經開始處理另外一個專案。
Mr. Kim has ________ started working on the other project.

5 此外，《真賦雜誌》已經開始對全體會員進行宣傳。
________, *True Gift Magazine* started advertising to its membership.

STEP 3 試題演練

請選出最適合填入空格的字詞。

1 Mr. Tran has not ------- moved to a new residential area near Brookline because of construction delays.

(A) never
(B) yet
(C) ever
(D) already

2 Ms. Jones has ------- proofread the article and is ready to send it to the publisher.

(A) but
(B) already
(C) still
(D) always

3 The employees who were recently hired have ------- visited the headquarters in New York.

(A) yet
(B) none
(C) never
(D) no

4 The consultants discovered that 20 percent of the employees ------- did anything productive last year.

(A) hard
(B) harder
(C) hardly
(D) hardest

03 須注意的副詞

STEP 1 題型觀摩

Q The newly built conference room in the Codex Center can accommodate ------- a hundred and fifty people.

(A) close by
(B) approximately
(C) near
(D) lately

Q 科德克斯中心新建造的會議室可容納將近 150 人。

(A) 附近
(B) 將近
(C) 接近
(D) 最近

答案 (B)

命題重點 「a hundred and fifty people」（150 人）為動詞的受詞，表達人的數量，因此空格填入修飾數字的副詞較為適當，答案應為 (B) approximately（將近、大約）。

1 與形容詞形態相同的副詞

以下的形容詞與副詞都是用同一個字來表示。有的字加上 -ly 會變成其他意思（請見下面的第 2 點），有的則變成不存在的字（如沒有 fastly 這個字）。

hard 困難的、堅硬的（形）— 努力地（副）	long 長的（形）— 長地（副）
fast 快速的（形）— 快速地（副）	near 鄰近的（形）— 鄰近地（副）
early 早的（形）— 早地（副）	yearly 每年的（形）— 每年地（副）
high 高的（形）— 高地（副）	enough 足夠的（形）— 足夠地（副）

The mattress from Helen Living is too **hard** for my back. 〔形容詞〕
海倫家飾公司的床墊對我的背來說太硬了。

The entire staff worked **hard** to meet the deadline. 〔副詞〕
全體員工都在努力工作趕上截止日。

2 副詞再加上ly，變成不同意思的副詞

hard 努力地	hardly 幾乎不……	close 靠近	closely 密切地、仔細地
late 遲地	lately 最近	most 大部分	mostly 大多、通常
high 高地	highly 高度地、非常	near 鄰近地	nearly 將近、大約
great 很好地	greatly 大幅地	just 僅僅	justly 公正地

Mr. Garcia sometimes comes to work **late**.
賈西亞先生有時上班會遲到。

I haven't talked to Mr. Pan **lately**.
我最近沒和潘先生說到話。

3 置於時間／數量／程度／距離前面的副詞

approximately 20 workers 將近 20 名工人	around 5:30 5 點 30 分左右
nearly 4 o'clock 將近 4 點	almost 12 items 幾乎有 12 個物品
about 3 hours 大約 3 小時	roughly 2 kilometers 大概 2 公里

Nearly three thousand people attended the job fair at Georgia University.
有將近 3000 人參加喬治亞大學的就業博覽會。

STEP 2 文法練習

請參考句子的中文意思，從提示字詞中選出適當的詞彙填入空格中，並選出該詞彙的詞性。

提示	enough	close	fast	closely	highly

1 書評們大力推薦安・泰勒的新書《機不可失》。
Critics ______________ recommended Ann Taylor's latest book, *Now or Never*.
（形容詞 | 副詞）

2 經理仔細審閱報告裡的數字。
The manager ______________ reviewed the figures in the report.
（形容詞 | 副詞）

3 訪客中心非常靠近公園的入口。
The visitor's center is very ______________ to the entrance of the park.
（形容詞 | 副詞）

4 某些東南亞國家的經濟突飛猛進。
The economy in some Southeast Asian countries is increasing ______________.
（形容詞 | 副詞）

5 這份與工作坊相關的計畫書含有充足的細節資訊。
The proposal concerning the workshop includes ______________ details.
（形容詞 | 副詞）

STEP 3 試題演練

請選出最適合填入空格的字詞。

1 Now that we have new regulations about the maximum working hours, we ------- ever work overtime.
(A) hard
(B) harder
(C) hardly
(D) hardest

2 The various cuisines that the restaurant recently introduced are good ------- to attract customers of different nationalities.
(A) enough
(B) nearly
(C) closely
(D) mostly

3 Experts say that the construction of the sports facilities in the city will take ------- a year to complete.
(A) closely
(B) around
(C) ever
(D) hardly

4 It is ------- to believe that some executives at the DK Corporation got involved in a bribery scandal.
(A) hard
(B) harder
(C) hardly
(D) hardest

多益實戰詞彙　副詞與近義詞

A 請熟記下列常見的副詞與其近義詞。

副詞	近義詞
approximately 將近、大約	nearly 將近、大約　around 大約　about 大約
frequently 經常	often 經常　repeatedly 反覆地
carefully 小心地、專心地	attentively 專心地　cautiously 謹慎地
periodically 定期地	regularly 規律地、定期地
rarely 很少、幾乎不	seldom 很少　hardly 幾乎不
typically 一般而言、通常	generally 一般而言　usually 通常
shortly 立刻、不久	soon 立刻、不久
fairly 非常、很	quite 很　pretty 非常　extremely 極度地
especially 尤其	particularly 尤其
initially 最初	first 最初
enthusiastically 熱心地	passionately 熱情地　eagerly 迫切地
swiftly 迅速地、快速地	quickly/rapidly/speedily/fast* 迅速地、快速地 *fast 形容詞副詞同形，沒有 fastly 這個字。
officially 正式地	formally 正式地
clearly 清楚地	obviously 明顯地
sufficiently 充足地	enough 足夠地　abundantly 充足地、豐富地 plentifully 充足地、豐富地

B 請選出與中文意思相符的詞彙（每題各有兩個正確答案）。

1 他的客戶離開後不久 → (shortly / soon / early) after his client left
2 定期跟朴先生見面 → meet Mr. Park (particularly / regularly / periodically)
3 一般而言需要十天 → (typically / usually / generally) takes 10 days
4 經常造訪紐約 → (nearly / frequently / often) visit New York
5 工作很忙碌 → (fairly / quite / extremely) busy with work
6 彼此幾乎沒有見面 → (obviously / hardly / rarely) see each other
7 正式宣布消息 → (formally / swiftly / officially) announce the news
8 最初被當作銀行使用 → (initially / often / first) used as a bank
9 專心聽演講者說話 → (carefully / attentively / generally) listen to the speaker
10 迅速抵達現場 → (swiftly / quickly / fairly) arrived on the scene

Practice Test 實戰演練

Part 5 請選出最適合填入空格的字詞。

1. The president and the vice president of the Medico Corporation ------- visit the offices in Eastern Europe.

   (A) nearly
   (B) occasionally
   (C) approximately
   (D) yet

2. Audience members must arrive on time because the theater doors will be closed ------- at 5 o'clock.

   (A) prompting
   (B) prompted
   (C) prompt
   (D) promptly

3. As the assembly line is not working -------, the management team is trying to determine the cause of the problem.

   (A) proper
   (B) properly
   (C) properness
   (D) propriety

4. Mr. Wong, who is ------- responsible for the Research Department, will take over as the chief executive.

   (A) soon
   (B) currently
   (C) still
   (D) nearly

5. All the members of the sales team were told that they must achieve ------- 80% of their monthly goals by the end of the week.

   (A) about
   (B) least
   (C) close
   (D) near

6. Online sales have ------- increased during the last twenty years because of the increasing numbers of Internet users.

   (A) dramatically
   (B) dramatic
   (C) dramas
   (D) drama

7. The company's new website has been functioning ------- since it underwent regular maintenance in December.

   (A) reliable
   (B) relies
   (C) relying
   (D) reliably

8. Ms. Lim has never been ------- for any company meetings, but she did not show up for the meeting this morning.

   (A) lately
   (B) late
   (C) lateness
   (D) being late

9. You are advised to read the instructions ------- before you press any of the buttons on the machine.

(A) careful
(B) carefully
(C) care
(D) cares

10. The new biscuits are slightly less sweet, ------- customers might not easily notice the difference.

(A) therefore
(B) so
(C) because of
(D) in spite of

11. The items in the warehouse are ------- wrapped for shipping to countries in the Middle East.

(A) individually
(B) accidently
(C) critically
(D) relevantly

12. The winner of the Chicago Music Festival Award will be ------- announced at 5 p.m. local time.

(A) especially
(B) promptly
(C) periodically
(D) typically

13. We are ------- pleased to announce that Ms. Chen will be promoted to senior financial analyst at our headquarters.

(A) very
(B) still
(C) already
(D) yet

14. The engineering team advises staff members to back up all of their computer files -------.

(A) attentively
(B) periodically
(C) individually
(D) exclusively

15. Demand for the new line of smartphones increased ------- after intensive advertising.

(A) shortly
(B) generally
(C) specifically
(D) relatively

16. The labor union officially announced that ------- 30 percent of the employees are currently working overtime.

(A) fairly
(B) quickly
(C) nearly
(D) sufficiently

Practice Test

Part 6 請先閱讀文章，再選出適合填入空格的內容。

Questions 17-20 refer to the following advertisement.

The Best Night's Sleep in Town

For the month of October, Country Breeze Bed & Breakfast will be offering huge discounts on our rooms to celebrate the coming of fall. We want to share our beautiful neighborhood with you, so let us help you with everything you need to observe the autumn leaves this year. We have a number of rooms that will be available for 45% off the normal room rate, which includes a free homemade meal each morning. -------(**17.**), all of our rooms have great views of the surrounding forest, and we provide free walking tours of the areas nearby. -------(**18.**). These rooms are going to fill -------(**19.**), so make your reservation today! You can visit us online at countrybreezebnb.com or call us at (345) 555-5517. We look forward to -------(**20.**) you soon!

17. (A) Additionally
(B) Addition
(C) For adding
(D) Additional

18. (A) Guests should bring their own bicycles to participate.
(B) Guests must book spots in advance because space is limited.
(C) Guests must pay an additional fee for this.
(D) Guests may park here.

19. (A) fast
(B) close
(C) near
(D) already

20. (A) meet
(B) meeting
(C) being met
(D) having been met

Part 7 請閱讀文章，並選出正確答案。

Questions 21-24 refer to the following flyer.

Richter Business School Community Speaker Series

Mr. Troy Baker

Senior Tax Advisor, Williams Accounting

The ABCs of Taxes for Individuals and Small Businesses

February 2, 7:00 p.m.

Cameron Hall

Nobody enjoys tax season. It seems like an impossible task to calculate everything each year. — [1] —. Some people don't even know where to start. Fortunately, our community speaker this month is a tax expert who knows everything about filing personal and small business taxes. — [2] —. Mr. Troy Barker, a tax accountant with over 20 years of experience, will show you how to easily file your taxes and introduce some online resources you can use to make the job easier. — [3] —. Audience members can ask more specific questions. Snacks and refreshments will be provided. — [4] —.

** *All presentations in the Community Speaker Series are open to students, faculty, and staff at the school as well as all other members of the community.*

21. What is Mr. Barker's presentation about?

(A) How to hire a tax accountant

(B) The services provided by Williams Accounting

(C) How to report one's annual taxes

(D) The new tax law that affects business school students

22. What is NOT mentioned about Mr. Barker?

(A) His work experience

(B) His current employer

(C) His field of expertise

(D) His contact information

23. In which of the position marked [1], [2], [3], and [4] does the following sentence best belong?

"The presentation will be followed by a Q&A."

(A) [1]

(B) [2]

(C) [3]

(D) [4]

24. What will be provided at the event?

(A) Free tax software

(B) Individual tax consultations

(C) Food and drinks

(D) A commemorative gift

Unit **10**

原級／比較級／最高級

Comparatives & Superlatives

01 原級

02 比較級

03 最高級

★ 多益實戰詞彙：比較級／最高級慣用語

★ 實戰演練

01 原級

STEP 1 題型觀摩

Q Sales clerks are required to answer customers' questions as ------- as possible.	Q 售貨員必須能盡可能立即回答顧客的問題。
(A) prompt	(A) 立即的（形容詞）、促使（原形動詞、現在簡單式）
(B) promptly	(B) 立即地（副詞）
(C) prompting	(C) 促使（現在分詞、動名詞）
(D) promptness	(D) 及時（名詞）
	答案 (B)

as 和 as 之間應填入形容詞或副詞原級，然後根據其修飾的內容，來決定要填入形容詞還是副詞。本題的空格用來修飾動詞「are required to」（必須……），應填入副詞，因此答案為 (B)。

1 原級的句型結構

as 和 as 之間要放入**形容詞或副詞**，也可以放入**限定詞 few / little / many / much 加上名詞**，是用**原級**來表達比較的概念。

as 形容詞／副詞 as ...	和……一樣（形容詞／副詞）
as many/much ＋名詞 as ...	和……一樣多（名詞）
as few/little ＋名詞 as ...	和……一樣少（名詞）

At my current job, I have to travel **as much as** I used to.
我目前的工作必須跟之前一樣常出差。

This product has **as many defects as** the previous model.
這項產品的缺點與之前的型號一樣多。

The good news is that we have received **as few complaints as** last year.
好消息是我們跟去年一樣，接到的申訴很少。

2 原級相關用法

the same 名詞 as ...	和……相同的（名詞）
twice as 形容詞／副詞 as ...	是……的兩倍（形容詞／副詞）
three times as 形容詞／副詞 as	是……的三倍（形容詞／副詞）

Unfortunately, we do not produce **the same model as** the one you have for the past few years.
很遺憾，我們已經不再生產跟您幾年前購得的型號相同的產品。

This week's maintenance is scheduled to take **twice as long as** last month's.
本週維護工程的時間，預計會是上個月維護時間的兩倍之久。

STEP 2 文法練習

請參考句子的中文意思，從提示字詞中選出適當的形容詞填入空格中，當中有幾題須改寫成副詞。

提示	many	precise	urgent	much	concerned

1 「珍妮花店」的售花量，與百貨公司裡的那家花店一樣多。
Jenny's Flower Shop sells ______________ flowers ______________ the one situated in the department store.

2 我一直和你一樣關心環境。
I am always ______________ you about the environment.

3 他們假設這個問題不像我們去年的問題一樣那麼緊急。
They assumed that this problem is not ______________ the one we had last year.

4 應徵者應該盡可能精確地回答問題。
Candidates should answer the questions ______________ they can.

5 我們今年花的錢是去年的兩倍。
This year, we have been spending twice ______________ money ______________ last year.

STEP 3 試題演練

請選出最適合填入空格的字詞。

1 You are advised to provide as ------- information as possible.
(A) detail
(B) details
(C) detailed
(D) more detailed

2 The research team has collected as ------- evidence as you requested.
(A) a lot
(B) much
(C) many
(D) little

3 We are so sorry for the inconvenience, and we promise your room will be cleaned as ------- as we can.
(A) quick
(B) quickly
(C) be quick
(D) quicker

4 Applicants' occupational backgrounds are as important ------- their educational achievements.
(A) as
(B) than
(C) more
(D) less

02 比較級

STEP 1 題型觀摩

Q The new system was far ------- complicated than everybody had anticipated. (A) more (B) as (C) much (D) most	Q 新系統遠比大家預想的更加複雜。 (A) 更（比較級） (B) 如此的（副詞） (C) 許多（原級） (D) 最（最高級〔須有 the〕） 答案 (A)

命題重點 本題屬於比較級考題類型。**形容詞有三個或更多音節時，須在單字前面加上 more 來形成比較級**。本題的形容詞 complicated（複雜的）後面接 than，由此可知空格要填入比較級 (A) more 作為答案。

1 比較級的結構

在單音節或兩個音節的形容詞／副詞後面加上 -er，三個音節以上的形容詞／副詞前面加上 more，即可形成比較級。要表達**「劣等比較」**（比……不……）時，則一律**在形容詞／副詞前面加上 less**。

Using public transportation is much **faster than** driving cars, especially during rush hour.
使用大眾運輸工具比開車還要快很多，尤其是在交通尖峰時段。

You should follow the directions **more carefully than** before.
你必須比以前更小心遵守規則。

The participants seemed to be **less interested** in the topic **than** before.
與會者似乎比較沒有像以前一樣，對這個主題那麼感興趣。

2 比較級相關用法

the ＋比較級 , the ＋比較級	愈……，愈……
much / even / still / a lot / far ＋比較級	遠比……很多
the ＋比較級 of the two	兩個之中較……的那一個

The more profit we make, **the more** taxes we are likely to pay.
我們賺愈多利潤，就有可能要繳愈多稅金。

The situation at the company was **much worse than** we had expected.
公司的處境遠比我們本來預想的糟很多。

What is **the more** convenient way **of** the two?
這兩個方法裡，哪一個方法比較方便？

STEP 2 文法練習

請參考句子的中文意思，從提示單字中選出適當的詞彙後，改寫成比較級填入空格中。

提示	experienced	seriously	high	much	expensive	complicated

1 我決定比以往更認真看待我的工作。
I decided to take my job ________________ ever before.

2 員工考核程序比我們原本想像的更加複雜。
The employee evaluation procedures were ________________ we had thought.

3 對電動車感興趣的人數，比五年前還要多。
The number of people interested in electric cars is ________________ it was 5 years ago.

4 新的電視廣告影片預計能為我們帶來更多營收。
The new TV commercial is expected to bring us ________________ revenue.

5 我們正在尋找更為低價的方式來推廣我們的產品。
We are looking for ________________ ways to promote our products.

6 這間旅行社正打算招募更有經驗的職員。
The agency is planning to recruit ________________ travel agents.

STEP 3 試題演練

請選出最適合填入空格的字詞。

1 Productivity at our factory is expected to increase as we are beginning to hire more workers ------- last year.

(A) as
(B) than
(C) that
(D) what

2 Home Furniture Co. will offer a ------- variety of items than before after its upcoming reopening.

(A) wide
(B) wider
(C) widest
(D) as wide

3 The new system will be able to predict the results ------- than the previous one.

(A) accurately
(B) accurate
(C) more accurate
(D) more accurately

4 The ------- you reply to our email, the more promptly we can take care of your problems.

(A) fast
(B) faster
(C) fastest
(D) be fast

03 最高級

STEP 1 題型觀摩

Q The bakery has a reputation for providing local residents with bread and cookies of the ------- quality.
(A) good
(B) better
(C) best
(D) well

Q 這間烘焙坊素以為當地居民提供最優質的麵包和餅乾而聞名。
(A) 良好的（形容詞原級）
(B) 更良好的（形容詞比較級）、更良好地（副詞比較級）
(C) 最良好的（形容詞最高級〔搭配 the〕）、最良好地（副詞比較級〔搭配 the〕）
(D) 良好地（副詞原級）

答案 (C)

命題重點 請務必確認空格前面是否有出現**定冠詞 the**，此為判別是否為**最高級**的方式。本題中，空格前面為定冠詞 the，因此答案為形容詞 good 的最高級 (C) best。

1 最高級的結構

在單音節或兩個音節的形容詞／副詞後面加上 -est，三個音節以上的形容詞／副詞前面加上 most，即可形成最高級。最高級前面要加上**定冠詞 the**。

the ＋最高級＋ of/among ＋團體	在……中最……的
the ＋最高級＋ in ＋地點	
the ＋最高級＋ of ＋時間	

Going to a local market is **the cheapest** way to enjoy the town.
前往當地市場，是遊覽此鎮最便宜的方式。

This is **the most luxurious** restaurant **in** this area.
這間是此區最奢華的餐廳。

August is **the hottest** month **of** the year.
8月是一年中最炎熱的月份。

2 最高級相關用法

the ＋最高級＋主詞＋ have ever ＋過去分詞	（動詞）過最……的……
one of the ＋最高級＋複數名詞	最……的之一
the ＋最高級＋ possible the ＋最高級＋ available	盡可能最……的 所能獲得的最……的

This is **the most creative** question **I have ever gotten**.
這是我所遇過最有創意的問題。

Sports agents help athletes to sign **the best contracts possible**.
運動經紀人會盡可能協助運動員簽下最優渥的合約。

STEP 2 文法練習

請參考句子的中文意思，從提示單字中選出適當的詞彙後，改寫成最高級填入空格中。

提示	practical	popular	good	old	demanding	experienced

1 在五名候選人中，我們會僱用最有經驗的一位。
Among the 5 candidates, we will hire ________________ one.

2 她是我合作過要求最為嚴苛的經理。
She is ________________ manager I've ever worked with.

3 我們會盡全力為您提供最優質的服務。
We will do our best to provide you with ____________ service ____________.

4 格林維爾藝術中心是本國歷史最為悠久的音樂廳之一。
The Greenville Center for the Arts is ________________ concert halls in the country.

5 這條健行步道是本區最受歡迎的觀光景點之一。
This hiking trail is ________________ tourist attractions in the area.

6 這是我參加過最為實用的研討會。
It was ________________ seminar I've ever been to.

STEP 3 試題演練

請選出最適合填入空格的字詞。

1 It was ------- informative presentation I have ever seen.

(A) most
(B) more
(C) the most
(D) the very

2 Of all the proposals we have received, we will choose the ------- cost-effective one.

(A) much
(B) more
(C) most
(D) best

3 Mountain Explorer, ever since it opened its first store in 1980, has been offering ------- variety of camping gear.

(A) wide
(B) wider
(C) widest
(D) the widest

4 I am convinced that Mr. Chin is by far the ------- lawyer in the field.

(A) competent
(B) more competent
(C) most competent
(D) competence

多益實戰詞彙　比較級／最高級慣用語

A 請熟記下列的高頻率比較級和最高級慣用語。

later today 今天稍晚的時候	at most 最多
later this week 本週稍晚的時候	as soon as possible 盡早
earlier today 今天稍早的時候	as quickly as you can 盡快
earlier this week 本週稍早的時候	as promptly as possible 盡量立刻
sooner or later 遲早	as often as needed 可視需求經常……
more than 超過……	the longest ever 史上最長／最久
less than 少於……	比較級＋ than expected/anticipated 比預期的更……
A rather than B A 而非 B	superior to 優於……
no longer 不再……	inferior to 劣於……
not any more 再也不……	senior to 比……高階／資深
no sooner than 不早於……、……之後	prior to 在……之前
no later than 不晚於……、……之前	prefer A to B 偏好 A 勝過 B
at least 至少	the most likely 最有可能
at the latest 最慢、最晚	would rather A than B 寧願 A 也不要 B

B 請選出與中文意思相符的詞彙。

1 超過 200 萬美元 → (more than / less than) 2 million dollars

2 偏好開車勝過搭飛機 → prefer driving (to / than) flying

3 比預期的更快 → faster (than / to) anticipated

4 盡量立刻 → as (prompt / promptly) as possible

5 最多 → at (most / last)

6 最慢、最晚 → at the (latest / last)

7 在會議之前 → (prior to / in advance) the meeting

8 遲早 → (sooner or later / rather than)

9 本週稍晚的時候 → (earlier / later) this week

10 本週五之前 → no (later than / faster than) this Friday

Practice Test 實戰演練

Part 5 請選出最適合填入空格的字詢。

1. The more features a cell phone has, the ------- customers are willing to pay.

   (A) many
   (B) much
   (C) most
   (D) more

2. You should finish your part of the work by Thursday at the ------- in order to meet the deadline.

   (A) late
   (B) later
   (C) latest
   (D) last

3. The blender you ordered is ------- available on the market as well as at our stores.

   (A) any more
   (B) no longer
   (C) more than
   (D) at least

4. Delta Electronics, one of the nation's ------- electric goods manufacturers, has decided to lay off more than 20% of its workforce.

   (A) large
   (B) larger
   (C) largest
   (D) largely

5. In order to get an additional discount, you are advised to place an order ------- Sunday, September 24.

   (A) no later than
   (B) at most
   (C) prior
   (D) in advance

6. A final decision about the merger will be made ------- this week.

   (A) late
   (B) later
   (C) latest
   (D) the latest

7. Since there have been major changes to the sales report, it will be completed ------- than planned.

   (A) late
   (B) later
   (C) latest
   (D) the latest

8. Ms. Shin is ------- dedicated teacher I've ever encountered in my whole life.

   (A) most
   (B) best
   (C) the most
   (D) the better

9. Repairing the old printer in the office would cost as ------- as getting a new one.

(A) even
(B) still
(C) very
(D) much

10. Mr. Rashid would rather spend more money ------- stay at a cheap hotel whose service he cannot be satisfied with.

(A) to
(B) before
(C) than
(D) more than

11. Researchers at World Cosmetics are trying to develop cosmetic products that are ------- harmful to the skin.

(A) little
(B) far
(C) less
(D) worse

12. The recently-developed ATD energy generator is reported to emit ------- more toxic materials than the previous one.

(A) many
(B) much
(C) a lot of
(D) very

13. Most of the respondents who participated in the survey seemed to prefer our older model ------- the new one.

(A) to
(B) than
(C) as well as
(D) more

14. A recent survey shows that the D2R dryer saves ------- much as the old model.

(A) two
(B) twice as
(C) twice
(D) second

15. In order for your order to be completed, your payment should be received by next Saturday at -------.

(A) late
(B) later
(C) latest
(D) the latest

16. Most people prefer to take express buses or trains even though they are more expensive ------- regular ones.

(A) as
(B) like
(C) than
(D) so

Practice Test

Part 6 請先閱讀文章，再選出適合填入空格的內容。

Questions 17-20 refer to the following memo.

Date: May 8
To: All Full-time Faculty
From: Administrative Office
Subject: Change in Printing Policy

Due to the increase in the prices of paper and ink, we will be implementing a new printing policy ------- (17.) this month. Currently, all full-time faculty members have ------- (18.) printing privileges. ------- (19.). This includes both color and black and white prints.

We apologize for any inconvenience. If you need ------- (20.) prints than your quota, you can add money to your printing account by asking Ms. Molly Baker, the administrative assistant. Funds can be added by cash only.

17. (A) late
(B) later
(C) latest
(D) the later

18. (A) unlimited
(B) anticipated
(C) prominent
(D) considerate

19. (A) This is too many pages to print for one person.
(B) However, starting next month, you will be limited to printing 250 pages per month.
(C) Additionally, part-time lecturers will be asked to only print in black and white.
(D) Therefore, most faculty members are wasting paper and ink.

20. (A) more
(B) most
(C) the most
(D) many

Part 7 請閱讀文章，並選出正確答案。

Questions 21-22 refer to the following article.

Farewell to a Piece of Wentzville

The Lakeford Diner will close its doors for good this Saturday after more than 60 years in business. First opened in 1955 by German immigrants Wilhelm and Ada Lamberts, the diner has become a local icon for its good food and classic interior. A special meal service will be held on the final day of business. It will feature a variety of dishes from across the diner's six decades of business. The current owner, who is a grandson of Wilhelm Lamberts, says that a steady decrease in business and the recent increase in rent were the primary reasons for having to shut down.

21. What is the purpose of the article?

(A) To announce a new restaurant opening

(B) To introduce the owners of a classic diner

(C) To inform the city that a local diner is going out of business

(D) To advertise a special meal service starting at the diner

22. Who is the current owner of the Lakeford Diner?

(A) The grandson of Wilhelm Lamberts

(B) Wilhelm Lamberts

(C) Ada Lamberts

(D) The city of Wentzville

Unit 11

連接詞

Conjunctions

01 名詞子句連接詞
02 對等／相關連接詞
03 從屬連接詞

★ 多益實戰詞彙：副詞
★ 實戰演練

01 名詞子句連接詞

STEP 1 題型觀摩

Q If the technical problem happens again, I recommend ------- you contact Mr. Sanders on the engineering team. (A) that (B) whether (C) if (D) since	**Q** 如果再發生技術問題，我建議您聯繫工程團隊的桑德斯先生。 (A)（引導名詞子句的連接詞） (B) 是否（引導名詞子句的連接詞） (C) 如果（從屬連接詞）、 是否（引導名詞子句的連接詞） (D) 自從、因為（從屬連接詞） **答案** (A)

該考題類型要選出最適當的名詞子句連接詞。空格後面的子句扮演動詞 recommend（建議）的受詞，由此可知該子句屬於名詞子句。此句的意思應為「建議『您做某件事』」較為適當，空格所引導的名詞子句為一個必須執行的行為，因此最好的答案為 (A) that。

1 that 引導的名詞子句（扮演主詞／受詞／補語）

主詞	**That** Mr. Han was late to work this morning is unusual. 韓先生今早遲到這情況很不尋常。
受詞	The report says **that** sales have increased for the last 2 years.〔當受詞時，that 可以省略〕 報告指出過去兩年銷售都有成長。
補語	The trouble is **that** we do not have enough time to finish it. 問題是，我們沒有充裕的時間來完成這件事。

2 whether / if 引導的名詞子句

主詞	**Whether** you will get a promotion hasn't been decided. 你會不會升職還沒有定論。
受詞	He asked me **whether/if** the new employee was adjusting well. 〔只有當受詞時，才可以用 if 引導名詞子句〕 他問我新進員工是否適應良好。
補語	The important thing is **whether** we are prepared to expand our business. 重要的是我們是否已經準備好擴展我們的業務範圍。

3 疑問詞引導的名詞子句

主詞	**What** you did is not acceptable. 你的所作所為讓人無法接受。
受詞	I don't know **who** will make a presentation tomorrow. 我不知道明天是誰要做簡報。
補語	That's **where** Mr. Williams started his first business. 這是威廉斯先生開創他第一個事業的地方。

★ 疑問詞 what / where / how / when / why / whether ＋不定詞 to V

My supervisor showed me **how to** access the intranet. (= how I should access the intranet)
我的主管示範怎麼連上內網給我看。

STEP 2 文法練習

請參考句子的中文意思，從提示字詞中選出適當的連接詞填入空格中，並選出該連接詞扮演的角色（提示字詞可重複選填）。

提示	that	whether	how	what

1 賈西亞先生問我們他需要為工作坊做什麼。
Mr. Garcia asked us ______________ he needed to do for the workshop.
（主詞｜受詞｜補語）

2 新進員工問我要怎麼做才能登入他的電子信箱。
The new employee asked me ______________ to access his email account.
（主詞｜受詞｜補語）

3 市長得決定我們是否要蓋新的社區中心。
The mayor has to decide ______________ we will build a new community center.
（主詞｜受詞｜補語）

4 這週是否動工還不確定。
______________ the construction will start this week is not certain yet.
（主詞｜受詞｜補語）

5 問題是，我們不能再資遣任何員工。
The problem is ______________ we cannot lay off any more employees.
（主詞｜受詞｜補語）

STEP 3 試題演練

請選出最適合填入空格的字詞。

1 The president is seriously considering ------- to expand to the Asia-Pacific market.

(A) what
(B) whether
(C) that
(D) either

2 The user's manual tells you ------- the dishwasher should be loaded and cleaned in detail.

(A) what
(B) that
(C) how
(D) if

3 The customer survey indicates ------- consumers are very happy with our products' quality.

(A) ever
(B) that
(C) where
(D) regarding

4 Public relations specialists teach you ------- to talk appropriately and politely in formal and informal settings.

(A) if
(B) whether
(C) how
(D) that

02 對等／相關連接詞

STEP 1 題型觀摩

Q To sign up for the training courses, you must ------- fill in the online registration form or visit the office on the second floor.

(A) either
(B) neither
(C) both
(D) not only

Q 要報名訓練課程，您必須上網填寫註冊表格，或去一趟二樓的辦公室。

(A) 要不……（要不……）（搭配相關連接詞 or）
(B) 既不……（也不……）（搭配相關連接詞 nor）
(C) 兩者都（搭配相關連接詞 and）
(D) 不只……（還有……）（搭配相關連接詞 but also）

答案 (A)

「either A or B」屬於相關連接詞用法，表示**「從兩種擇一」**的概念。一般我們會觀察選項和題目句來找出適當的連接詞。但本題空格後面出現連接詞 or，表示前面應搭配 either 使用，因此答案為 (A)。

1 對等連接詞

對等連接詞能夠**連接兩個單字、片語或子句**，置於句子的中間，表達**對等關係**。

對等連接詞的種類和例句	
and 和、而且	pilots **and** flight attendants 機師和空服員
or 或者	left it on the table **or** in the cabinet 把它放在桌上或櫃子裡
but 但是	spacious **but** noisy 寬敞但吵雜
so 所以	I worked overtime, **so** I felt tired. 我加班，所以感覺很疲倦。

The conference was very useful, **but** there was not a Q&A session. 〔連接子句和子句〕
這場會議很有用，但沒有問答時間。

2 相關連接詞

相關連接詞會與 both / either 等字詞搭配使用。

相關連接詞的種類和例句	
both A and B A 和 B 兩者都……	**both** Kim **and** Jung 金和鄭兩人都……
either A or B A 或 B 兩者之一、要不 A 要不 B	**either** tomorrow **or** Friday 要不明天要不星期五
neither A nor B 兩者都不、既不 A 也不 B	**neither** close **nor** comfortable 既不近也不舒適
not only A but (also) B 不只 A 還有 B = B as well as A〔強調的重點為 B〕	**not only** smart **but also** beautiful 不只聰明也很漂亮 = beautiful **as well as** smart

★ **相關連接詞連接主詞時，動詞的單複數與 B 主詞一致；但是「both A and B」只能使用複數動詞。**

Either the CEO **or** the executives **interview** the candidates.
〔動詞單複數與 B = the executives 一致〕
要不是執行長，要不就是高層來對應徵者進行面試。

Both managers **and** staff members **are** advised to attend the meeting. 〔僅能用複數動詞〕
建議經理和員工都要出席會議。

STEP 2 文法練習

請參考句子的中文意思，從提示字詞中選出適當的詞彙填入空格中。

提示	neither	and	or	either	both

1 裝配線和倉庫都因為施工而關閉。
______________ the assembly line and the warehouse are closed for construction.

2 庫柏先生和希爾先生都不同意在該地區蓋游泳池。
______________ Mr. Cooper nor Mr. Hill agreed to build a swimming pool in the area.

3 工廠訪客須配戴護目鏡和安全帽。
Those who visit the factory must wear protective goggles ______________ a safety helmet.

4 勞倫茲女士將在 3 月 1 日或 2 日的其中一天做簡報。
Ms. Lorentz will give a presentation on either March 1 ______________ 2.

5 想拿到折價券的話，可以上我們官網或向我們的員工索取。
To get a discount coupon, you can ______________ visit our website or ask someone on our staff.

STEP 3 試題演練

請選出最適合填入空格的字詞。

1 The National Modern Museum will close during April ------- May because it will refurbish its exhibition rooms.

(A) and
(B) but
(C) on
(D) or

2 ------- the market research report or the budget report will be discussed in the meeting.

(A) Either
(B) Neither
(C) Both
(D) Not only

3 Neither Mr. Simpson ------- Ms. Kelly volunteered to work on Saturday to prepare for the visit of the regional manager.

(A) but
(B) nor
(C) or
(D) and

4 Consumers were impressed ------- with the quality of the new cosmetics but also with the reasonable prices.

(A) both
(B) either
(C) not only
(D) neither

03 從屬連接詞

STEP 1 題型觀摩

Q	Q
------- you want to access your online billing statement, you have to create an online account first. (A) Even if (B) If (C) That (D) Unless	如果您想取得網路帳單，則必須先建立一個網路帳戶。 (A) 雖然、即使（從屬連接詞） (B) 如果（從屬連接詞）、 是否（引導名詞子句的連接詞） (C)（引導名詞子句的連接詞） (D) 除非（從屬連接詞） 答案 (B)

命題重點 空格連接兩個子句，由此可知需要填入連接詞，此時請先確認句子的意思，選出最適當的連接詞。空格所在的子句表達「如果」較為適當，因此答案為連接詞 (B) If。

1 表時間／原因／讓步的從屬連接詞

時間	when 當…… since 自從	while 當…… as soon as 一……就……	until 直到 before 在……之前	once 一旦 after 在……之後
原因	because/as/since 因為、由於		now that 既然、由於	
讓步	although/though 雖然、儘管 while 儘管、然而		even though / even if 雖然、即使	

2 表條件／目的／結果的從屬連接詞

條件	if / provided / providing / as long as 如果、只要	unless 除非
目的	so that ＋主詞＋ can 如此（主詞）就可以……	
結果	so ＋形容詞／副詞＋ that 如此地（形容詞／副詞）以致於……	

If (= **Provided** / **Providing** / **As long as**) I get help from my colleagues, I can complete this report.
我如果能得到同事的協助，就能完成這份報告。

3 從屬連接詞與介系詞

	連接詞	介系詞
時間	while 當……　before 在……之前	during/for 在……期間　prior to 在……之前
原因	because 因為	because of 因為（＋名詞）
條件	unless 除非	without / but for 要不是、若非
讓步	although 雖然	in spite of (= despite) 儘管（＋名詞）

Because the weather was terrible, the company picnic was canceled.〔連接詞＋主詞＋動詞〕
→ **Because of** the terrible weather, the company picnic was canceled.〔介系詞＋名詞〕
因為天氣不佳，公司野餐取消了。

STEP 2 文法練習

請參考句子的中文意思，從提示字詞中選出適當的連接詞填入空格中。

提示	since	that	although	unless	because

1 馬路看起來十分擁擠，所以我們決定搭大眾運輸。
The road looked so crowded ---------------- we decided to use public transportation.

2 雖然摩爾女士很努力嘗試，但還是沒能趕上截止期限。
---------------- Ms. Moore tried hard, she couldn't meet the deadline.

3 除非我們擴大店面，否則無法陳列更多商品。
---------------- we expand the store, we cannot display any more products.

4 金先生從 20 歲開始就在這家公司工作，直至今日。
Mr. Kim has been working for this company ---------------- he was 20 years old.

5 因為威廉斯先生明天沒空，所以會議延期了。
---------------- Mr. Williams is not available tomorrow, the meeting has been postponed.

STEP 3 試題演練

請選出最適合填入空格的字詞。

1 Mr. Hunt, the president of Weber Retail, has decided to lay off a few employees ------- he has to reduce labor cost.

(A) what
(B) whether
(C) that
(D) since

2 ------- you need any technical assistance with software issues, please feel free to contact us at any time.

(A) If
(B) That
(C) After
(D) Whether

3 ------- Wilson Industries needs Mr. Wong for the New York office, they will transfer him to the Asian branches next year.

(A) That
(B) Who
(C) Although
(D) Even

4 ------- the company enhanced the new website, Uptown Design customers will be able to view their history of recent orders.

(A) Although
(B) Because
(C) If
(D) Even if

多益實戰詞彙 副詞

A 請熟記下列的高頻率副詞。

thoroughly 徹底地	extensively 廣泛地
frequently 頻繁地	attentively 專心地、周到地
previously 以前	promptly 立即地、迅速地
relatively 相對地	consistently 一致地、始終如一地
gradually 逐漸地	efficiently 有效率地
finally 終於	accurately 精確地
primarily 主要地	punctually 準時地
immediately 立即	temporarily 臨時地
mutually 互相地	sparingly 謹慎地、保守地
closely 密切地、仔細地	fairly 相當、非常
specifically 特別地、明確地	cordially 熱誠地、誠摯地
conveniently 方便地	typically 典型地
dramatically 戲劇性地	completely 完整地
exclusively 專門地、排外地	equally 相同地、同樣地
extremely 極其、非常	properly 恰當地、正確地
adversely 敵對地、不利地	accordingly 相應地
readily 容易地、樂意地	reasonably 合理地

B 請選出與中文意思相符的詞彙。

1 下午 3 點準時離開 → leave (primarily / promptly) at 3 p.m.

2 徹底檢查這幅畫 → examine the painting (fairly / thoroughly)

3 始終批評該項計畫 → (closely / consistently) criticize the plan

4 逐步提高產能 → (gradually / equally) increase productivity

5 主要負責活動 → (primarily / mutually) responsible for the event

6 價格合理的飯店 → a(n) (exclusively / reasonably) priced hotel

7 地點方便的建築 → a (conveniently / completely) located building

8 專心聆聽 → listen to it (cordially / attentively)

9 僅限會員使用 → available (adversely / exclusively) to members

10 準時完成工作 → complete the job (properly / punctually)

Practice Test 實戰演練

Part 5 請選出最適合填入空格的字詞。

1. ------- registration is quite low, the technology workshop scheduled for November 1 will be canceled.

(A) As
(B) Until
(C) Though
(D) That

2. Mr. Parker offers clients ------- personal loans and business loans at low interest rates.

(A) either
(B) both
(C) neither
(D) even

3. Mr. James Hamilton, the president of KBest Technology, is seriously considering ------- to renew the contract with Muhammad Patel.

(A) because
(B) that
(C) what
(D) whether

4. TK Max Clothing guarantees delivery within 4 business days, ------- my order arrived even more quickly.

(A) but
(B) so
(C) because
(D) despite

5. Ms. Sapp is ------- sure that some of the employees will be transferred to the new branch office in Manchester.

(A) typically
(B) exclusively
(C) fairly
(D) mutually

6. Eric's Dining has requested ------- we inform them of the number of guests no later than Tuesday.

(A) so
(B) if
(C) and
(D) that

7. If you want deals available ------- to Gold members of the Ocean Fitness Club, sign up now.

(A) relatively
(B) exclusively
(C) efficiently
(D) accordingly

8. The clients from Fred & Frank Co. arrived ------- at the office to sign the contract with us.

(A) punctually
(B) thoroughly
(C) gradually
(D) primarily

9. Sales of the new products increased ------- due to the improved designs and reasonable prices.

(A) drama
(B) dramatically
(C) dramatic
(D) being dramatic

10. ------- the company executives interviewed Mr. Freeman, they all agreed to hire him as the chief financial officer.

(A) After
(B) Provided
(C) Although
(D) Unless

11. Not only the coordinator ------- also the instructors attended the workshop on classroom management.

(A) but
(B) and
(C) so
(D) or

12. We make sure that the air pollution levels in the city are ------- monitored.

(A) closely
(B) nearly
(C) dramatically
(D) adversely

13. Solar energy is becoming a key factor in Europe ------- investment in nuclear power plants is declining.

(A) when
(B) while
(C) for
(D) but

14. When we receive instructions from headquarters, we will act -------.

(A) readily
(B) accordingly
(C) equally
(D) frequently

15. *Black Dog* won the critics' award for best documentary at the Paris Movie Festival ------- it was chosen as the audiences' least favorite movie.

(A) therefore
(B) nevertheless
(C) since
(D) although

16. DHO employees have to inform their immediate supervisor by 9:30 ------- they expect to miss a day of work.

(A) only
(B) if
(C) even
(D) so

Part 6 請先閱讀文章，再選出適合填入空格的內容。

Questions 17-20 refer to the following article.

The 14th annual IT and New Enterprises Conference took ------- (17.) last weekend at the Sierras Hotel in Madrid. The conference brought together over 9,000 IT professionals and entrepreneurs from around the world to participate in workshops and to network with one another. ------- (18.). In addition, IT startup expert Travis Goldman was scheduled to give a presentation, ------- (19.) it was canceled because his flight was delayed due to the weather. Overall, most professionals considered the event to be another ------- (20.).

17. (A) place
(B) placed
(C) placing
(D) places

18. (A) Admission to the event was included in a membership to the monthly newsletter.
(B) New technology was showcased throughout the conference.
(C) The keynote speech was given by the president of NextBit Technology, Sarah Tran.
(D) The local government helped to host the event this year.

19. (A) but
(B) so
(C) therefore
(D) nonetheless

20. (A) success
(B) factor
(C) composition
(D) result

Part 7 請閱讀文章，並選出正確答案。

Questions 21-23 refer to the following web page.

www.toysgalore.com

Toys Galore

HOME | **NOTICES** | LOCATIONS | SHOPPING | CONTACT

We would like to inform our customers that there will be a temporary change in our hours of operation starting this Monday, December 8. During the holiday season, we will be open for extended hours to facilitate all of your shopping needs. Our new temporary hours will be 7:00 a.m. to 11:30 p.m. daily. This change is only for the 7th Street location of Toys Galore. All other locations will maintain their normal business hours. The 7th Street store will resume its normal business hours in January. We hope that this change will help make the holiday season a bit easier for you all. If you would like more information, please call (777) 765-7654.

21. For whom is this notice most likely intended?

(A) Customers

(B) Business partners

(C) Employees

(D) Maintenance workers

22. The word "facilitate" in line 3 is closest in meaning to

(A) install

(B) process

(C) support

(D) appoint

23. What will happen in January?

(A) A store location will be changed.

(B) A store's hours will return to normal.

(C) A special holiday event will begin.

(D) A new store will be opened.

Unit 12

關係詞
Relatives

01 關係代名詞

02 關係代名詞的省略／介系詞+關係代名詞

03 關係副詞／複合關係詞

★ 多益實戰詞彙：形容詞片語

★ 實戰演練

Unit 12

01 關係代名詞

STEP 1 題型觀摩

Q The technician, ------- started working a few weeks ago, informed us that he would like to quit the job.

(A) which
(B) what
(C) who
(D) whom

Q 幾週前才上工的技術人員跟我們說他想辭職。

(A) ……的東西（表示事物的主／受格關係代名詞）
(B) ……的東西（表示事物的複合關係代名詞）
(C) ……的人（表示人的主／受格關係代名詞）
(D) ……的人（表示人的受格關係代名詞）

答案 (C)

命題重點 當空格前面為先行詞、後面連接結構不完整的子句時，該考題考的就是**關係代名詞**。本題中，先行詞為人「the technician」（技術人員），而空格後面連接動詞，因此答案為表示人的主格關係代名詞 (C) who。

1 關係代名詞是什麼？

兩個句子中出現意思相同的名詞時，會省略後出現的名詞，改用關係代名詞連接兩個句子。**關係代名詞後面連接不完整的子句，形成關係子句。**

The employee will be able to enjoy a day off.
\+ **The employee** won first prize in the competition.
→ The employee **who*** won first prize in the competition will be able to enjoy a day off.
贏得比賽第一名的員工將能休一天假。

*關係代名詞代替主詞「the employee」（員工），因此使用表示人的主格關係代名詞 who。

2 關係代名詞的種類

確認關係代名詞所代替的名詞屬於主格、受格或是所有格，並判別先行詞為人還是事物。

先行詞	主格	受格*	所有格
人	who	who(m)	whose
事物、動物	which	which	whose / of which
人+事物／動物	that	that	-

*受格關係代名詞可以省略。

We often go to the seafood restaurant **that/which** is located in Chinatown.
〔先行詞+主格關係代名詞+動詞〕
我們常去位於中國城的海鮮餐廳。

The people **(whom/that)** I work with are all reliable.
〔先行詞+受格關係代名詞+主詞+動詞〕
和我一起工作的那些人全都值得信賴。

Mr. Lee, **whose** house is currently being renovated, is staying with us temporarily.
〔先行詞+所有格關係代名詞+名詞〕
目前房子正在裝修的李先生暫時和我們住在一起。

STEP 2 文法練習

請參考提供的中文，並使用適當的關係代名詞連接下方的兩個句子。

1 「樸實有機商店」販售當地種植的有機蔬果。
❶ Down-to-Earth stores sell organic fruits and vegetables.
❷ The fruits and vegetables are grown in local areas.
→ ____.

2 這家工廠生產的產品大多出口到其他國家。
❶ Most of the products are exported to other countries.
❷ Most of the products are produced in this factory.
→ ____.

3 考績不佳的員工將不符合領年終獎金的資格。
❶ Employees will not be eligible for an annual bonus.
❷ The employees' performance reviews were not very good.
→ ____.

4 該職位將不考慮遲交的應徵資料。
❶ The applications will not be considered for the position.
❷ The applications were received too late.
→ ____.

STEP 3 試題演練

請選出最適合填入空格的字詞。

1 There were more than a hundred of people ------- were interested in the job fair.
(A) who
(B) which
(C) whose
(D) of which

2 Masco's is an organization ------- mission is to help those who are less privileged.
(A) who
(B) whose
(C) that
(D) what

3 Any contracts ------- are not signed by the president will not have any legal standing.
(A) that
(B) whose
(C) what
(D) whom

4 Candidates ------- job experience is extensive will be likely to get a job at the company.
(A) who
(B) whom
(C) whose
(D) of which

02 關係代名詞的省略／介系詞＋關係代名詞

STEP 1 題型觀摩

Q Mr. Evans participated in the company workshop, ------- which he learned about how to deal with financial programs.

(A) of
(B) from
(C) with
(D) during

Q 伊凡斯先生參加了公司的工作坊，從中他學習到如何處理財務計畫。

(A) ……的（介系詞）
(B) 從……（介系詞）
(C) 與……（介系詞）
(D) 在……期間（介系詞）

答案 (D)

本題測驗的是能否選出適當的介系詞，放在關係代名詞前面。根據題意，「他參加了工作坊，『在工作坊進行期間』學到很多東西」較為適當，因此代替 workshop（工作坊）的 which 前面最適合填入 (D) during。

1 關係代名詞的省略

(1) 受格關係代名詞可以省略。

Christina is an employee (that/whom) I can always rely on when I have computer problems.
克里斯蒂娜向來是我遇到電腦問題時可以仰賴的員工。

(2) 主格關係代名詞 who / which / that 可以與後面的 be 動詞一起省略，變成**分詞形態**。

The person (who is) <u>working</u> on the construction project is my coworker Sam.
處理這項建案的人是我的同事山姆。

Decisions (that/which were) <u>made</u> at the meeting are supposed to be kept confidential.
會議上所做的決議應當保密。

(3) 如果關係代名詞前面有逗號，則為「**非限定用法**」（描述的對象只有一個，只是補充說明），**關係代名詞不可以省略**，而且**只能用 who(m) / which，不可以用 that**。

The workers, who (, that [X]) had finished their work, left early today.
那些工人已經完成了工作，（因此）今天比較早走。

2 介系詞＋關係代名詞

在關係子句中，先行詞扮演介系詞的受詞角色時，可將介系詞移至關係代名詞前面。但須注意，**移到前面的介系詞只能用 whom（人）或 which（東西），不可以用 that**。

There will be a board meeting.

+ The directors will discuss some ways to promote products <u>during the board meeting</u>.

→ There will be a board meeting, during which (during that [X]) the directors will discuss some ways to promote products.

董事會即將召開，在此期間董事們將討論推廣產品的幾項做法。

STEP 2 文法練習

請參考提供的中文，並使用適當的關係代名詞連接下方的兩個句子。

1 我們即將主打的產品是我們的新洗碗機。
❶ We are going to focus on the product.
❷ The product is our new dishwasher.
→ ______________________________.

2 你困擾時應該談談的人是諾里斯先生。
❶ You need to talk to the person when you are in trouble.
❷ The person is Mr. Norris.
→ ______________________________.

3 你得寄信給應徵者才行，他們的姓名寫在最後一頁。
❶ The names of the applicants are written on the last page.
❷ You have to send a letter to the applicants.
→ ______________________________.

4 當地製造的電器產品通常比進口的便宜。
❶ The electric products are usually cheaper than the imported ones.
❷ The electric products are produced in local areas.
→ ______________________________.

STEP 3 試題演練

請選出最適合填入空格的字詞。

1 The 4-digit product code ------- in the box is necessary when you try to get your product repaired.
(A) show
(B) shown
(C) showing
(D) to show

2 The highway ------- two major cities is always crowded with cars and trucks.
(A) connect
(B) connecting
(C) connected
(D) to be connected

3 The lawyer ------- you recommended the other day failed to get the job at the firm.
(A) that
(B) what
(C) whose
(D) which

4 A high turnover rate at the company has always been an issue ------- everybody is concerned.
(A) which
(B) about which
(C) about that
(D) that

03 關係副詞／複合關係詞

STEP 1 題型觀摩

Q The convention center, ------- the annual sales meeting will be held, is located on Birmingham Street.

(A) which
(B) who
(C) where
(D) wherever

Q 舉辦年度銷售會議的會議中心位於伯明罕街。

(A) ……的東西（表示事物的主／受格關係代名詞）
(B) ……的人（表示人的主／受格關係代名詞）
(C) ……的場所（表示場所的關係副詞）
(D) 無論何處（複合關係副詞）

答案 (C)

本題要懂得分辨**關係代名詞與關係副詞的差異**。在關係子句中，省略的對象為名詞時，要使用關係代名詞；省略的對象為副詞時，則要使用關係副詞。觀察關係子句的部分，結束在「... will be held」（將會被舉辦），後面應有表示場所的副詞片語「in the convention center」（在會議中心）但被省略，因此空格要填入表示場所的關係副詞 (C) where。

1 關係副詞

關係副詞用來連接兩個句子，省略其中一個具有相同意義的副詞或副詞片語。有別於關係代名詞引導的子句，**在關係副詞引導的子句中，關係副詞後面要連接結構完整的句子**。

This is **the office**. + You can get your passport issued **in the office**.

→ This is the office **where***you can get your passport issued.
您可以辦護照的地點就是這間辦公室。

*此處由 where 所引導的關係子句，用來修飾先行詞「the office」（辦公室）。

	先行詞	關係副詞		先行詞	關係副詞
地點	the place / the city 等	where	原因	the reason	why
時間	the time / the year 等	when	方法	the way	how

2 複合關係詞

關係代名詞或關係副詞的字尾加上 -ever，會形成**複合關係代名詞**或**複合關係副詞**。

複合關係代名詞		複合關係副詞	
whoever	無論是誰	whenever	無論何時
whatever	無論什麼	wherever	無論何處
whichever	無論哪個	however*	無論如何

*however 有兩個意思：(1) 轉折副詞「然而」、(2) 複合關係副詞「無論如何」。

Whoever is interested in overseas training should submit an application.
無論是誰，只要想去海外訓練都應提出申請。

Whenever you need help, you can come to the manager's office.
每逢您需要幫助時，都可以到經理辦公室來。

STEP 2 文法練習

請參考提供的中文，並使用適當的關係詞連接下方的兩個句子。

1 我建議您去一下那間您可以重辦簽證的辦公室。
I recommend you visit the office ______________ you can get your visa issued again.

2 春末是我們客戶意圖購買夏季商品的高峰期。
Late spring is the season ______________ our customers try to purchase our summer items.

3 辦公用品您可以上網或到實體店面訂購，看哪個對您比較方便。
You can order office supplies online or offline, ______________ is more convenient for you.

4 希望他們能夠解釋配送延誤這麼久的原因。
Hopefully, they will be able to explain the reason ______________ the delivery was so delayed.

5 無論是誰，只要參加這項調查都能免費得到一張甜點優待券。
______________ participates in the survey will be able to get a free dessert coupon.

6 奢侈品不管有多貴，仍受到 20 至 40 歲的女性族群歡迎。
______________ expensive they may be, luxury goods are very popular among women aged from 20 to 40.

STEP 3 試題演練

請選出最適合填入空格的字詞。

1 The sales report indicates that we sold much more during the month ------- prices were lowered.

(A) when
(B) whenever
(C) what
(D) how

2 Anyone ------- makes an online purchase this month will be able to get a 20% discount.

(A) who
(B) whom
(C) whenever
(D) whoever

3 There will be a Q&A session ------- we will address some of your concerns.

(A) where
(B) which
(C) whom
(D) that

4 Among the candidates, ------- has the most experience will get the job.

(A) wherever
(B) however
(C) whichever
(D) whoever

多益實戰詞彙 形容詞片語

A 請熟記下列的高頻率形容詞片語。

be comparable to 與……相當	be appreciative of 對……感激
be exempt from 豁免於……	be popular with/among 受……歡迎
be central to 對……至關重要	be proficient in 擅長……、精通……
be considerate of 對……體貼、替……著想	be representative of 作為……的代表
be entitled to 享有……的資格／權力	be anxious about 為……感到焦慮
be qualified for 符合……的資格	be skilled at 擅長……
be responsible for 對……負責、負責……	be hopeless at 非常不擅長……
be responsive to 對……積極應對	be different from/than 和……不同
be beneficial to 對……有益	be similar to 和……類似
be rude to 對……無禮	be the same as 和……相同
be nice to 對……友好	a wide range of 各式各樣的……
be grateful for 對……感激	a significant number of 大量的……
be thankful for 對……感激	a considerable amount of 大量的……
be ready for 準備好要做……	a wide variety of 各式各樣的……
be necessary for 對……有需要	be apt to 適合做……
be open to 對……開放	be uncertain about 對……感到不確定
be certain about 對……感到確定	be concerned about 對……關切、擔心……

B 請選出與中文意思相符的詞彙。

1 對他人體貼 → be (considerate / considerable) of others

2 各式各樣的電子產品 → a (very / wide) variety of electronic goods

3 對長者無禮 → be rude (to / of) the elderly

4 對顧客的需求積極應對 → very (responsible / responsive) to customers' needs

5 免除稅金 → be (exempt / except) from taxes

6 很受青少年歡迎 → be (comparable / popular) with teenagers

7 大量受訪者 → a (significant / comparable) number of respondents

8 ……為改進所需的 → be necessary (for / about) the improvements

9 精通英語 → be (beneficial / proficient) in English

10 全天 24 小時對外開放 → be (open / apt) to anyone 24 hours a day

Practice Test 實戰演練

Part 5 請選出最適合填入空格的字詞。

1. You will be assigned to a mentor ------- will give you more training on how to use the software.

(A) whom
(B) who
(C) whoever
(D) whose

2. Office Yard has a(n) ------- variety of office furniture and supplies that you need when you start a new business.

(A) wide
(B) significant
(C) indifferent
(D) representative

3. Safety clothes should be worn by anyone ------- duties involve working in the plant.

(A) who
(B) whose
(C) of which
(D) how

4. Ms. Han, who has been with the company for more than a decade, is ------- for the position of regional manager.

(A) qualify
(B) qualifying
(C) qualified
(D) qualifications

5. Many of the food critics described the restaurant as a place ------- you can feel the homiest atmosphere.

(A) whom
(B) which
(C) what
(D) where

6. The size of this parking structure is ------- to that of the country's largest one, which was recently built.

(A) compared
(B) comparable
(C) comparison
(D) comparing

7. The software ------- was installed on our computers seem to be working fine.

(A) that
(B) where
(C) what
(D) of which

8. Mega Health Club, which recently opened in the downtown area, is ------- to its members' requests.

(A) responsive
(B) respective
(C) interested
(D) concerned

9. Some of the executives said that they were ------- about the effects of the new TV commercial.

(A) available
(B) capable
(C) uncertain
(D) unwilling

10. It's Mr. Yang's responsibility to handle technical problems ------- we have a problem with the computers.

(A) which
(B) however
(C) whenever
(D) that

11. A recent survey shows ------- customers are willing to spend more money if good quality and services are guaranteed.

(A) that
(B) which
(C) what
(D) whatever

12. Ms. Davis, ------- was seriously injured in the accident, was sent to the hospital.

(A) who
(B) that
(C) whoever
(D) which

13. It is important to be ------- of the assistance you get from your coworkers.

(A) grateful
(B) subject
(C) comprehensive
(D) appreciative

14. We are supposed to hold some training sessions ------- you can get more information about the procedure.

(A) where
(B) which
(C) what
(D) that

15. The company is looking for someone who is ------- for the rapidly changing environment.

(A) reliable
(B) ready
(C) accustomed
(D) independent

16. Anyone ------- would like to take part in the workshop should sign up in advance.

(A) who
(B) whoever
(C) whatever
(D) whom

Part 6 請先閱讀文章，再選出適合填入空格的內容。

Questions 17-20 refer to the following letter.

Kitchen Works USA
456 Port Smith Lane

Dear Sir or Madam,

I am writing to request a full refund on a blender ------- **17.** I recently bought from your company. I bought this blender on a recommendation, but after using it for the first time, I found several unacceptable problems.

First, the blender ------- **18.** to hold 2.0 liters, but it can only hold 1.5 liters when blending. Next, when I opened the package, I noticed ------- **19.** the lid was cracked before I even used it. -------. **20.** I am honestly very disappointed with the product and would not recommend it to anyone. Please let me know how to continue with the refund process.

Sincerely,
Thomas Fraser

17. (A) whichever
(B) which
(C) of which
(D) what

18. (A) advertised
(B) was advertising
(C) was advertised
(D) advertisement

19. (A) that
(B) which
(C) whatever
(D) how

20. (A) Furthermore, it is extremely loud when being used.
(B) However, my friend suggested I buy this blender.
(C) On top of that, I no longer have the receipt.
(D) This is the only issue I have with the product.

Part 7 請閱讀文章，並選出正確答案。

Questions 21-22 refer to the following job advertisement.

The Sky Is the Limit at LBG Pharmaceuticals

Are you looking for a career that has unlimited potential for growth? Do you have experience in competitive sales? If so, then Florida-based LBG Pharmaceuticals is looking for you!

We are looking for a full-time senior sales coordinator for our Washington, D.C. branch. The position involves setting and achieving monthly sales goals, working directly with high profile B2B clients, and leading projects to increase sales efficiency. The senior sales coordinator will also collaborate with the sales team to achieve these goals.

We offer a competitive salary with extra pay based on individual and team sales. We will consider experience in the salary offer, and applicants with a background in the pharmaceutical or medical fields are greatly preferred. Medical insurance and a severance package are provided to all full-time employees.

To apply, visit our website at LBGpharm.com/jobs. Applicants need to provide an email address and three professional references. If you have any questions regarding the application process, feel free to contact us as 809-555-1234.

21. What duty of a senior sales coordinator is mentioned in the ad?

(A) Achieving sales goals on a monthly basis

(B) Competing with other salespeople

(C) Studying medicine and pharmaceuticals

(D) Driving between Florida and Washington, D.C.

22. What benefit is NOT provided to full-time employees?

(A) Health insurance

(B) A severance pay

(C) A company car

(D) A bonus based on sales

Unit 13

介系詞

Prepositions

01 表時間／表地點的介系詞

02 其他介系詞／易混淆介系詞

03 介系詞的慣用語

★ 多益實戰詞彙：介系詞用法（1）

★ 實戰演練

01 表時間／表地點的介系詞

STEP 1 題型觀摩

Q The technology career fair, where more than 30 companies in the field are expected to participate, will be held ------- Tuesday, March 15.

(A) at
(B) on
(C) in
(D) by

Q 預計有 30 多家公司參加的科學技術就業博覽會，將舉辦在 3 月 15 日星期二。

(A) at
(B) on
(C) in
(D) by

答案 (B)

命題重點 本題要選出適當的介系詞。空格後面連接「日期」，因此必須使用介系詞 on，故答案為 (B)。請務必一併熟記與時間和地點相關的介系詞。

1 表示時間的介系詞

at ＋時刻／明確的時間點	on ＋星期幾／日期／平日／週末	in ＋月份／季節／年度／上午／下午／晚上
at 3 p.m. 下午 3 點時 **at** midnight 午夜時 **at** lunchtime 午餐時	**on** Friday 在週五 **on** March 1 在 3 月 1 日 **on** weekdays 在平日	**in** October 在 10 月 **in** the summer 在夏天 **in** 1945 在 1945 年

2 表示時間點或一段時間的介系詞

時間點	一段時間
since March 自從 3 月起 **by** Monday 到週一之前 **until** 7 a.m. 直到早上 7 點 **before / prior to** the departure 啟程前	**for** 3 hours 為時三小時 **during** the meeting 會議期間 **throughout** the year 整年、全年 **within** 3 days 在三天內

3 表示地點的介系詞

at ＋地點（機場／車站）	on ＋表面（街道／樓層／物品／名單）	in ＋空間之內（城市／國家／大陸）
at the airport 在機場 **at** the bus stop 在公車站牌	**on** Pine Street 在派恩街上 **on** the first floor 在一樓 **on** the top shelf 在最上層架子上	**in** the meeting room 在會議室 **in** Seoul 在首爾 **in** Asia 在亞洲

4 表示方向或位置的介系詞

方向	位置
to 到⋯⋯　from 從⋯⋯ into 到⋯⋯裡面　out of 從⋯⋯出來 across from / opposite 在⋯⋯對面 along 沿著⋯⋯　past 經過⋯⋯	between A and B 在 A 和 B 之間 above 在⋯⋯上方　below 在⋯⋯下方 over 在⋯⋯（正）上方　under 在⋯⋯（正）下方 in front of 在⋯⋯前面　behind 在⋯⋯後面 next to 在⋯⋯旁邊

STEP 2 文法練習

請參考句子的中文意思，從提示字詞中選出適當的介系詞填入空格中。

提示	on	during	at	prior to	in

1 門羅先生會去機場接英格蘭來的客戶。
Mr. Munroe will pick up the clients from England ______________ the airport.

2 調查用的問卷在你桌上。
The questionnaires for the survey are ______________ your desk.

3 開會時火災警報器誤響了。
A false fire alarm went off ______________ the conference.

4 荷里斯女士打算明年在洛杉磯開一家新分店。
Ms. Hollis plans to open a new branch office ______________ Los Angeles next year.

5 拉倫斯基女士在休假前必須把成本估計完。
Ms. Larensky must complete the cost estimate ______________ her vacation.

STEP 3 試題演練

請選出最適合填入空格的字詞。

1 The appointment of a new chief financial officer will be announced ------- the conference room.

(A) at
(B) on
(C) in
(D) to

2 The opening ceremony for the children's health clinic will begin ------- 10 o'clock tomorrow morning.

(A) at
(B) on
(C) in
(D) into

3 The London National Museum will be closed for renovations beginning ------- September 2.

(A) at
(B) on
(C) in
(D) for

4 The office furniture for the new staff members is scheduled to be delivered ------- Thursday.

(A) at
(B) on
(C) in
(D) out of

02 其他介系詞／易混淆介系詞

STEP 1 題型觀摩

Q Parking on Edison Street will be banned for the next few weeks ------- road repairs. (A) regarding (B) because of (C) in spite of (D) so that	**Q** 愛迪生街因為道路維修，未來幾週將禁止停車。 (A) 關於（介系詞） (B) 因為（介系詞） (C) 儘管（介系詞） (D) 所以（從屬連接詞） 答案 (B)

命題重點 空格位在名詞「road repairs」（道路維修）的前面，應填入介系詞。根據本句話的意思，填入 (B) because of，表示無法停車的「原因」最為適當。

1 表示原因／讓步／主題的介系詞

原因（因為、由於）	讓步（儘管）	主題（關於）
because of / due to / owing to / thanks to / on account of 例 due to increased costs 因為成本增加	**in spite of / despite / notwithstanding** 例 despite the conflicts 儘管發生衝突	**about / on / regarding / in regard to / with regard to / concerning** 例 regarding the policy 關於這項政策

2 表示手段／方法／工具／目的／比較／資格的介系詞

手段／方法／工具	目的	比較／資格
by bus 搭公車 **by** email 用電子郵件 **with** the key 用鑰匙	**for** the project 為了該專案	**like** last year 像去年 **unlike** last month 不像上個月 **as** president 作為董事長

3 易混淆介系詞

by vs. until	**for vs. during**（在……期間）	**between vs. among**（在……之間）
submit **by** Monday 週一前交 wait **until** 7 p.m. 等到晚間 7 點為止	**for** 3 years 三年之久 **during** the winter 冬季期間	**between** Kelly and Tom 在凱莉和湯姆之間 **among** the colleagues 在同事之間
by：在……之前、到……的時候（表結束的概念） until：直到……（表持續的概念）	for ＋數字 during ＋表期間的名詞	between：在兩者之間 among：在三者以上之間

STEP 2 文法練習

請參考句子的中文意思，從提示字詞中選出適當的介系詞填入空格中。

提示	for	notwithstanding	during	due to	by

1 每個人都必須到 201 號室參加每月例會。
Everybody is required to come to Room 201 ______________ the monthly meeting.

2 會議期間，金先生的手機響了三次以上。
______________ the meeting, Mr. Kim's phone rang more than three times.

3 我們必須在 7 月 1 日前再聘僱一位行政人員。
We need to hire another administrative worker ______________ July 1.

4 研討會因為報名不踴躍而將停辦。
______________ low registration, the workshop will be canceled.

5 儘管有一些重大問題，公司去年度的表現還是很成功。
______________ some serious problems, the company had a successful year.

STEP 3 試題演練

請選出最適合填入空格的字詞。

1 The meeting ------- the museum's operations will be postponed and rescheduled for Wednesday afternoon.

(A) despite
(B) regarding
(C) owing to
(D) in order to

2 ------- the reception, the CEO introduced the newly appointed director of marketing to the employees.

(A) So
(B) During
(C) For
(D) To

3 Naomi Apparel is well known in the fashion industry ------- a trendsetter for women's clothing.

(A) by
(B) as
(C) to
(D) with

4 Applicants must submit a résumé and a cover letter ------- email.

(A) by
(B) until
(C) for
(D) on

03 介系詞的慣用語

STEP 1 題型觀摩

Q To prevent any technical problems, all employees are required to update their system ------- a regular basis.

(A) at
(B) on
(C) in
(D) to

Q 為避免任何技術問題發生，全體員工都必須定期更新系統。

(A) at
(B) on
(C) in
(D) to

答案 (B)

「on a regular basis」（定期地）屬於介系詞的慣用語，故答案為 (B)。只要知道這個用法，本題就能輕鬆選出答案。請熟記下方常考介系詞慣用語，會對解題非常有幫助。

慣用的介系詞用法

at	on	in
at a low cost 以低廉的成本 **at** the beginning 一開始 **at** the end 最後 **at** the speed of 以……的速度 **at** no extra charge 不需額外費用	**on** the list 在名單／清單上 **on** sale 特價中 **on** foot 徒步 **on** duty 工作中 **on** arrival 抵達時 **on** a regular basis 定期地 **on** time 準時 **on/upon** receipt of 收到……時	**in** advance 提前、事先 **in** public 在公開場合 **in** general 一般而言 **in** a timely manner 省時、有效率 **in** yellow 黃色地 **in** time 及時 **in** the end (= finally) 最終地
under	**within**	**from / to**
under construction 興建中、施工中 **under** warranty 在保固期內 **under** the contract 根據合約 **under** the agreement 根據協議	**within** walking distance 在步行距離內 **within** the limit 在限制範圍內 **within** the organization 在組織內部	**from** a distance 從遠方 **from** one's point of view 依（某人的）觀點 key/solution **to** ……的關鍵／解決辦法
for	**above / below**	**by**
for free 免費 **for** safety reasons 出於安全考量 **for** sale 出售	**above** one's expectations 超乎（某人的）預期 **above/below** average 在平均水準之上／下	**by** three dollars （增加／減少）3 美元 **by** the manager 由經理（做……） **by** fax 透過傳真

STEP 2 文法練習

請參考句子的中文意思，從提示字詞中選出適當的介系詞填入空格中。

提示	within	under	at	on	in

1 令女士有信心能有效率地完成專案。
Ms. Ling is confident that she will complete the proposal ______________ a timely manner.

2 新辦公室在我們目前辦公室的步行距離內。
The new office is ______________ walking distance of our current one.

3 電腦還在保固期內，所以可以免費修理。
The computer can be fixed for free because it is ______________ warranty.

4 飯店賓客能待到下午 5 點，不會被收取額外費用。
Hotel guests can stay till 5 p.m. ______________ no extra charge.

5 他們在候補名單上找不到田中洋子這個人。
They couldn't find Yoko Tanaka ______________ the waiting list.

STEP 3 試題演練

請選出最適合填入空格的字詞。

1 The government workers have been working overtime to review all the budget reports ------- time.
(A) at
(B) on
(C) in
(D) by

2 The items will be shipped within 3 to 4 business days ------- receipt of your order.
(A) as
(B) upon
(C) by
(D) for

3 Since Marin Restaurant is very crowded on the weekend, you are advised to book a table ------- advance.
(A) at
(B) on
(C) in
(D) for

4 Mr. Costa was not able to handle the assigned task ------- a prompt manner.
(A) at
(B) on
(C) in
(D) within

多益實戰詞彙 介系詞用法（1）

A 請熟記下列的高頻率介系詞用法。

due to 因為……	except (for) 除了……之外
in terms of 就……方面來說	in exchange for 作為……的交換
depending on 依賴……、依……而定	regardless of 無論……
as a result of 由於……	thanks to 由於……、幸虧……
in response to 作為對……的答覆	in an effort to 努力……
on the basis of 以……的基礎	in light of 有鑑於……
in conjunction with 與……一起	as to 至於……
up to 接近於……、多達……	in cooperation with 和……合作
in charge of 負責……	on account of 由於……
on behalf of 代表……	along with 與……一起
in comparison with 與……相比	instead of 代替……、而不是……
in favor of 贊成……、有利於……	contrary to 違背……、與……相反
on top of 除了……之外還……	as of 從……起
aside from 除了……之外	in celebration of 為了慶祝……
apart from 除了……之外	by means of 藉著……方法或手段
such as 例如……、像是……	in honor of 紀念……、向……表示敬意
in addition to 除了……之外還……	as part of 作為……的一部分

B 請選出與中文意思相符的詞彙。

1 為了慶祝財務長新官上任 → in (cooperation / celebration) of the new financial chief

2 與我們競爭對手相比 → in (addition / comparison) with our competitors

3 例如地點和價格 → (such as / depending on) the location and the price

4 除了它的高品質以外 → (on top of / as a result of) its great quality

5 負責管理行銷團隊 → (in charge of / in light of) the marketing team

6 從 10 月 21 日起生效 → effective (as to / as of) October 21

7 多達百分之 40 → (as of / up to) 40 percent

8 幸虧有您的資助 → (apart from / thanks to) your financial support

9 除了有八折的折扣之外 → (in addition to / in terms of) a 20-percent discount

10 至於錢的問題 → (as to / as of) money problems

Practice Test 實戰演練

Part 5 請選出最適合填入空格的字詞。

1. ------- Ms. Thompson has been with the company for only a year, she has already taken on a lot of high-profile projects.

(A) Although
(B) In spite of
(C) Without
(D) Unless

2. ------- November 1, the new law regarding the maximum number of hours of overtime employees can work will go into effect.

(A) As of
(B) As to
(C) With
(D) Regarding

3. ------- the competition from big chain stores, Anderson Shop has maintained its popularity with customers.

(A) Despite
(B) Until
(C) Though
(D) In case of

4. ------- the winter, the government facilities will be open for residents in the area.

(A) With
(B) Regarding
(C) At
(D) Throughout

5. ------- our recent expansion, the CEO has decided to hire more employees by the end of the month.

(A) As of
(B) Due to
(C) Such as
(D) Despite

6. Although the company is based in Europe, its production facilities are all ------- Vietnam.

(A) at
(B) on
(C) in
(D) to

7. To place an order, you can either send the order form ------- fax or visit our website.

(A) at
(B) by
(C) in
(D) to

8. We store office supplies in the copy room ------- the vending machines on the first floor.

(A) into
(B) across from
(C) down
(D) throughout

9. The Franklin Theater is now showing the play *The Bright Night*, and it will run ------- March 15.

(A) until

(B) by

(C) at

(D) between

10. ------- the chief financial officer, Mr. Turner will directly report to the company president.

(A) By

(B) As

(C) Even

(D) So

11. Mr. Brown was disappointed to find out that he was not ------- consideration for the upcoming promotion.

(A) under

(B) about

(C) before

(D) over

12. The flight to Chicago has been canceled ------- inclement weather conditions.

(A) though

(B) because

(C) due to

(D) in spite of

13. ------- an emergency, you must not use the elevators in the building but use the stairs.

(A) So as

(B) In case of

(C) Although

(D) In spite of

14. Employees are allowed to work ------- 42 hours a week as a result of the new policy on working conditions.

(A) except for

(B) such as

(C) up to

(D) apart from

15. The executives started discussing the merger and acquisition ------- themselves before the CEO came into the room.

(A) between

(B) among

(C) about

(D) over

16. Ms. Camp has to file the expense report for her trip to Shanghai ------- March 1.

(A) by

(B) at

(C) about

(D) nearly

Practice Test

Part 6 請先閱讀文章，再選出適合填入空格的內容。

Questions 17-20 refer to the following information.

Beaverton Central Library

The Beaverton Central Library offers service to any resident of Beaverton County and to members of the Greater Oregon Library Network. Our materials on loan include books, multimedia (DVD, Blu-ray, music CDs, and audio books), and daily laptop rentals. We also provide research support for any members who need help finding materials ------- (17.) a specific topic. Library members can also reserve classrooms for group studying, and we have one conference room available as well. These are rented ------- (18.) a first-come, first-served basis, so please contact us in advance to check availability. ------- (19.).

The library is open every day from 9:00 a.m. ------- (20.) 8:00 p.m. and is closed on national and state holidays. For more information about events or other library services, please visit our website at www.belib.com.

17. (A) at
(B) on
(C) in
(D) to

18. (A) of
(B) on
(C) within
(D) to

19. (A) This can be done by phone or online on our web page.
(B) Late fees will accumulate daily for unreturned materials.
(C) Our many community events include both adult and youth programs.
(D) These also include several books related to the requested research topic.

20. (A) to
(B) of
(C) as
(D) and

Part 7 請閱讀文章，並選出正確答案。

Questions 21-25 refer to the following schedule and email.

Digital Marketing Conference Schedule

SATURDAY

10:00 a.m.	Opening Ceremony
10:30 a.m.	Keynote Speaker: "The Future of the Online Marketplace" / Kevin Heart
1:30 p.m.	Workshop: "Social Media Management" / Ashley Kumar
4:00 p.m.	Day One Summary / Claire Bach, Conference Chairperson
5:30 p.m.	Formal Dinner / Main Conference Hall

SUNDAY

11:00 a.m.	Presentation: "Multimedia Advertisement Theory" / Rosella Aguilar
3:00 p.m.	Workshop: "Using Mobile Platforms" / Dr. Orion Akbar
6:30 p.m.	Conference Closing Ceremony
7:00 p.m.	Dinner
8:30 p.m.	Networking Cocktail Event

All meals and beverages will be provided by the hotel's dining facilities.

From:	Orion Akbar
To:	Claire Bach
Subject:	Conference Schedule

Dear Mrs. Bach,

Thanks again for the opportunity to host a workshop at the conference this year. Unfortunately, my flight returning home is on Sunday night, so I have to leave the conference immediately after my workshop ends. However, I will be able to attend all of the events before then. I want to let you know so that you can plan accordingly. Thanks for understanding, and I'm sorry for any inconvenience this might cause.

Sincerely,

Orion Akbar, PhD
Department of Marketing
Tulsa State University

21. What event will be held on Sunday morning?

(A) Ms. Aguilar's presentation
(B) The opening ceremony
(C) Mr. Akbar's workshop
(D) Mr. Heart's keynote presentation

22. What is NOT indicated on the conference schedule?

(A) There will be two workshops during the conference.
(B) Food will be provided at the conference.
(C) The event takes place over two days.
(D) Admission must be paid in advance.

23. Why did Mr. Akbar email Mrs. Bach?

(A) To request a change in a schedule
(B) To cancel his workshop
(C) To inform her of his personal schedule
(D) To register for the conference

24. What most likely is Mr. Akbar's job?

(A) Event organizer
(B) Professor
(C) Conference manager
(D) Social media marketer

25. What event will Mr. Akbar NOT be able to attend?

(A) The opening ceremony
(B) The keynote presentation
(C) The networking cocktail event
(D) Ms. Kumar's workshop

Unit 14

假設語氣

The Subjunctive Mood

01 與現在事實相反／與過去事實相反

02 與未來事實相反／混合型假設語氣

03 假設語氣倒裝句

★ 多益實戰詞彙：介系詞用法（2）

★ 實戰演練

01 與現在事實相反／與過去事實相反

STEP 1 題型觀摩

Q If Mr. Park were willing to help us with the final report, we ------- it in before the deadline.

(A) will turn
(B) would turn
(C) would have turned
(D) was turning

Q 如果朴先生願意幫我們做決算報告，我們就能趕在期限前繳交。

(A) 將繳交（未來簡單式）
(B) 將繳交（would ＋原形動詞）
(C) 將已繳交（would ＋ have ＋ p.p.）
(D) 正在繳交（過去進行式〔第一／三人稱單數〕）

答案 (B)

看到連接詞 if 及後面的過去簡單式動詞 were，可知本題屬於「與現在事實相反」的假設語氣用法。**if 子句中使用過去簡單式動詞，主要子句則要用「would ＋原形動詞」**，因此答案為 (B) would turn。

1 與現在事實相反

假設現在沒有發生的事情時，會使用「與現在事實相反」的假設語氣。雖然句子所表達的概念為「現在」，但是請注意 **if 子句必須使用過去簡單式動詞**。

if 子句	主要子句
If ＋主詞＋過去簡單式動詞（例：were / had / went）	主詞＋ would / could / might ＋原形動詞

If we informed them of the schedule change, they would not need to leave so early.
如果我們（現在）跟他們說行程有異動，他們（現在）就不用這麼早離開。

If the books were*in stock, we could send them to you right away.
如果書（現在）有庫存，我們（現在）就能馬上寄給您。

*與現在事實相反的的假設語氣中，if子句中be動詞的過去簡單式一律用were。

2 與過去事實相反

假設過去沒有發生的事情時，會使用「與過去事實相反」的假設語氣。雖然句子所表達的概念為「過去」，但是請注意 **if 子句必須使用過去完成式動詞**。

if 子句	主要子句
If ＋主詞＋過去完成式動詞 （例：had been / had gone）	主詞＋ would / could / might ＋ have ＋ p.p.

If we had had enough time, we would have done more research on it.
如果我們（當初）時間充裕，我們（當初）就能把它研究得更透徹。

If the real estate agent had shown me a different apartment, I would not have decided to move here.
如果房仲（當初）有讓我看另一間公寓，我（當初）就不會決定搬來這裡。

STEP 2 文法練習

請先閱讀題目句，再參考提供的中文例子套入假設語氣用法，改寫成意思相同的句子。

1 He didn't take a morning flight, so he couldn't make it to the meeting.
→ 如果他搭了早上的班機，他就能趕上會議。
If he ______________, he ______________ to the meeting.

2 There are not enough staff members, so we need to work overtime frequently.
→ 如果職員人數夠，我們就不用常常加班了。
If there ______________, we ______________ overtime frequently.

3 You don't drive to work frequently, so you don't spend a lot of money on commuting.
→ 如果你常常開車去上班，你就會花很多錢在通勤上。
If ______________ frequently, you ______________ on commuting.

4 I didn't order the shelf last month, so I didn't get a better deal.
→ 如果我上個月下訂那個櫃子，就能用更便宜的價格買到。
If I ______________ last month, I ______________ a better deal.

5 I didn't find the class boring and useless, so I didn't complain to the coordinator.
→ 如果我當初覺得那門課既無聊又沒用，早就跟助教反映了。
If I ______________, I ______________ to the coordinator.

6 I didn't know about the defect in the product, so I was not more careful when dealing with it.
→ 如果我當初知道那個產品有缺陷，處理時就會更加小心了。
If I ______________ in the product, I ______________ when dealing with it.

STEP 3 試題演練

請選出最適合填入空格的字詞。

1 If the team ------- the renovation project earlier, they would have finished it before the reopening.
(A) starts
(B) started
(C) has started
(D) had started

2 If I had not ------- given the information, I would not have figured out what the problem was.
(A) be
(B) being
(C) been
(D) was

3 If the staff had not worked so hard, the project ------- up as a complete failure.
(A) ended
(B) have ended
(C) had ended
(D) would have ended

4 If he ------- the chairman of the company, he would bring much more radical changes to the organization.
(A) elected
(B) were elected
(C) have been elected
(D) had elected

02 與未來事實相反／混合型假設語氣

STEP 1 題型觀摩

Q If I ------- up all night last night, I would not be able to concentrate on this work now.

(A) stays
(B) stayed
(C) have stayed
(D) had stayed

Q 如果我昨晚熬夜一整晚，現在就無法專心做這件工作了。

(A) 熬夜（現在簡單式）
(B) 熬夜（過去簡單式）
(C) 熬夜（現在完成式）
(D) 熬夜（過去完成式）

答案 (D)

命題重點 根據句中出現的「時間點」，可以判斷題目是否要使用「混合型假設語氣」。本題的 if 子句中出現「last night」（昨晚），主要子句中則使用 now（現在），**兩個子句的時態並不一致，由此可知該句話屬於混合型假設語氣**。從屬子句為過去時間，因此答案為過去完成式 (D) had stayed。

1 現在可能的假設（一般條件句）

if 子句的動詞時態為現在簡單式，主要子句則要使用助動詞 will / can / may 等。用來描述**發生可能性極高的狀況**。

if 子句	主要子句
If ＋主詞＋現在簡單式動詞	主詞＋ will / can / may ＋原形動詞

If it **rains** tomorrow, the company retreat **will be** postponed.
如果明天下雨，公司野餐將會延期。

2 與未來事實相反的假設（可能性極小）

用於可能會發生，但**發生的可能性極小的狀況**。

if 子句	主要子句
If ＋主詞＋ should ＋原形動詞	– 主詞＋ will / can / may ＋原形動詞 – 祈使句

If you **should encounter** any problems with this product, **feel** free to contact one of our sales representatives.
您在使用這項產品時萬一碰到任何問題，儘管和我們任何一位業務代表聯絡。

3 混合型假設語氣

將「與過去事實相反」的假設結合「與現在事實相反」的假設，形成混合型假設語氣。因此，if 子句要使用過去完成式；主要子句則要使用「would ＋原形動詞」。

if 子句	主要子句
If ＋主詞＋過去完成式	主詞＋ would / could / might ＋原形動詞

If they **had put** more effort into creating a package design, the book **would be** selling more now.
如果他們（當初）更努力設計包裝，這本書現在可能賣得更好。

STEP 2 文法練習

請參考句子的中文意思，並使用括號內的動詞完成句子。

1 要是你當初早點開始弄專案，我們現在可能就已經完成了。
If you ________________ the project sooner, we ________________ be finished with it by now. (start)

2 如果你的傷勢惡化，就得去看醫生。
If your injury ________________, you will have to see a doctor. (get worse)

3 要是我昨晚值夜班，我現在可能會很累。
If I ________________ on the night shift last night, I ________________ tired now. (work / be)

4 萬一您對應徵程序還有任何疑問，請造訪我們官網。
If you ________________ any further inquiries about the application process, please visit our website. (have)

5 如果班機延誤，你就得找家機場飯店過夜才行。
If the flight ________________, you ________________ have to stay at one of the hotels at the airport. (be delayed)

6 要是醫生當初有警告我這種藥的危險性，我現在可能就沒事了。
If the doctor ________________ me of the danger of the medicine, I ________________ any problems now. (warn / not have)

STEP 3 試題演練

請選出最適合填入空格的字詞。

1 If management had informed the employees of the problem, we ------- better prepared for the crisis now.

(A) will be
(B) would be
(C) would have been
(D) have been

2 If you ------- your order before 2 p.m., your purchase will be delivered to your home the next day.

(A) place
(B) places
(C) placed
(D) had placed

3 If you ------- experience any difficulties accessing your account, please contact the customer service center.

(A) will
(B) should
(C) would
(D) might

4 If Mr. Chang ------- us with the design, we would not be ready to give a presentation now.

(A) has not helped
(B) does not help
(C) had not helped
(D) have not helped

03 假設語氣倒裝句

STEP 1 題型觀摩

Q Had she ------- the employee of the year, everybody at the company would have been very surprised.

(A) chosen
(B) was chosen
(C) been chosen
(D) be choosing

Q 如果被選為年度最佳員工的是她，公司裡的每個人都會很驚訝。

(A)（被）選擇（過去分詞）
(B) 被選擇（過去簡單式被動語態〔第三人稱單數〕）
(C) 被選擇（被動語態〔過去分詞形態〕）
(D) 正在選擇（進行式〔原形動詞形態〕）

答案 (C)

命題重點 假設語氣用法中，省略 if 後，將主詞和動詞交換位置，便形成倒裝句。上方題目句原本的句子應為被動語態：「If she had been chosen . . .」（如果她被選為……），省略 if 後，再將 had 和 she 交換位置，後面的「been chosen」不變，因此空格適合填入的動詞形態為 (C) been chosen。

1 「與現在事實相反」的假設語氣倒裝句

若為「與現在事實相反」的假設，先省略 if 子句中的 if，再將主詞和動詞交換位置。但請注意，if 子句的動詞為 were 或 had（有）時才可以倒裝。

~~If~~ **I were** you, I would take that offer.

→ **Were I** you, I would take that offer.

如果我是你的話，我就會接受那個工作邀約。

~~If~~ **I had** a desire to be a manager, I would go back to school to get an MBA.

→ **Had I** a desire to be a manager, I would go back to school to get an MBA.

如果我想當上經理，我就會重回校園攻讀企管碩士。

2 「與過去事實相反」的假設語氣倒裝句

若為「與過去事實相反」的假設，先省略 if 子句中的 if，再將主詞和助動詞 had 交換位置。

~~If~~ **I had known** that the company is losing so much money, I wouldn't have invested in its stock.

→ **Had I known** that the company is losing so much money, I wouldn't have invested in its stock.

如果我（當初）知道這家公司虧損這麼嚴重，我（當初）就不會投資這支股票了。

3 「與未來事實相反」的假設語氣倒裝句

若為「與未來事實相反」的假設，先省略 if 子句中的 if，再將主詞和助動詞 should 交換位置。

~~If~~ **you should have** any further questions about the procedure, feel free to ask me at any time.

→ **Should you have** any further questions about the procedure, feel free to ask me at any time.

萬一您對程序還有任何疑問，請隨時問我別客氣。

STEP 2 文法練習

請參考句子的中文意思，並使用括號內的動詞完成句子，接著再改寫成倒裝句。

1 如果車沒壞，我們早就準時到了。
If the car ________________, we ________________ there right on time. (break down / get)
→（省略 if 改寫）________________.

2 如果不是您一直以來的幫忙，我們現在恐怕無法維持公司運作。
If it ________________ not for your consistent support, we ________________ maintain our business. (be / will be able to)
→（省略 if 改寫）________________.

3 如果公車在尖峰時段不要那麼擁擠，我就不用開車去上班了。
If the buses ________________ less crowded during rush hour, I ________________ to work. (be / not drive)
→（省略 if 改寫）________________.

STEP 3 試題演練

請選出最適合填入空格的字詞。

1 ------- the HR Department announced the training session sooner, more people would have participated in it.

(A) If
(B) Have
(C) Had
(D) Whether

2 ------- Ms. Sanderson not busy with other projects, she would be willing to help us.

(A) Were
(B) Had
(C) Had been
(D) If

3 ------- Mr. Cooper participated in the conference, he would have met a lot of professionals in his field.

(A) If
(B) Had
(C) Have
(D) Should

4 ------- you experience any difficulty accessing your bank account, you may want to reset your password.

(A) If
(B) Should
(C) Unless
(D) So long as

多益實戰詞彙 介系詞用法（2）

A 請熟記下列的高頻率介系詞用法。

at all times 總是	in any case 無論如何
at no extra charge 不需額外費用	in consequence of 由於……
on schedule 在時程上	in stock 有現貨、有庫存
behind schedule 進度落後	out of stock 無現貨、無庫存
ahead of schedule 進度超前	upon request 一經要求
in detail 詳細地	as a token of 作為……的表示
in advance 提前、事先	in the end 最後、終於
in effect 生效	in case of 假使……、萬一……
in accordance with 根據……、與……一致	in the event of 假如發生了……
in terms of 就……方面來說	out of town 出遠門
according to 根據……	out of order 失序
at the beginning of 在……開始時	on time 準時
at the end of 在……結束時	just in time 及時
as a result 結果、因此	in contrast to 和……形成對比
as opposed to 與……相反	contrary to 與……相反、違背……

B 請選出與中文意思相符的詞彙。

1 努力減少成本 → in (an effort / an effect) to reduce costs

2 進度落後 → (ahead of / behind) schedule

3 有鑑於之前的研究 → in (terms / light) of previous research

4 萬一在緊急情況下 → (in case / in the end) of emergency

5 作為感激的表示 → (as a result of / as a token of) one's gratitude

6 與他的說詞相反 → (contrast to / contrary to) his explanation

7 學期末 → (at the end of / at the last of) the semester

8 就銷售數字方面來說 → (in terms of / in accordance with) sales figures

9 除了一些錯誤以外 → (apart from / according to) a few mistakes

10 簡報開始時 → (at the first / at the beginning) of the presentation

Practice Test 實戰演練

Part 5 請選出最適合填入空格的字詞。

1. If Maxim & Co. ------- in the company, it would not be having such serious financial problems now.

(A) does not invest
(B) has not invested
(C) had not invested
(D) was not invested

2. As ------- to their initial plan, they decided to build an additional cafeteria for those who have a hard time finding a place to eat.

(A) opposed
(B) result
(C) effect
(D) order

3. If Mr. Wood ------- more attention to his employees, such a large number of people would not be trying to leave his department.

(A) has paid
(B) had paid
(C) has been paying
(D) pays

4. Please note that the change in the policy will be ------- effect as of tomorrow morning.

(A) in
(B) from
(C) out of
(D) at

5. If you want to take maternity leave, you should officially submit a form -------.

(A) prior
(B) at least
(C) before
(D) in advance

6. We regret to inform you that the wireless printer you ordered is currently ------- stock.

(A) in
(B) out of
(C) from
(D) not

7. If the technical team ------- additional training last month, they would be much more familiar with the new system.

(A) receives
(B) received
(C) had received
(D) has received

8. ------- you have any further questions, please feel free to contact our customer service center.

(A) Unless
(B) Should
(C) As long as
(D) As well

9. Thanks to the help of a forwarder, the shipment is expected to arrive in the country ------- schedule.

(A) ahead of
(B) in advance
(C) prior to
(D) after

10. If the printer ------- properly, you should read the manual provided before you call a repairman.

(A) do not work
(B) does not work
(C) did not work
(D) had not work

11. ------- you need extra stationery while studying here, do not hesitate to ask our secretary for more.

(A) Were
(B) What
(C) Should
(D) Had

12. During this promotion period, you can check out late ------- no extra charge.

(A) for
(B) in
(C) at
(D) from

13. We are trying to incorporate more recreational activities ------- to improve employee morale.

(A) in an effort
(B) out of order
(C) in terms
(D) with regard

14. ------- you want to find more detailed information about the area, please refer to the booklet placed on the table.

(A) Whether
(B) If
(C) That
(D) What

15. An original copy of your transcript will be made available ------- request.

(A) from
(B) in
(C) upon
(D) according to

16. If you ------- an express delivery service, the product you requested would be here now.

(A) used
(B) had used
(C) have used
(D) would use

Practice Test

Part 6 請先閱讀文章，再選出適合填入空格的內容。

Questions 17-20 refer to the following information.

The Food for All Foundation has announced that it will be -------(17.) a new homeless shelter in North Stonebrook. The shelter will include a fully operational soup kitchen and will provide sleeping space for 120 people. There are also plans to -------(18.) a job counseling service to help individuals looking for work. Construction on the new facility will begin this March. -------(19.). This construction was made possible due to a substantial donation from an anonymous donor. If this donation -------(20.) made, we would not be starting this project.

17. (A) open
(B) opened
(C) opening
(D) to open

18. (A) implement
(B) apply
(C) enclose
(D) relinquish

19. (A) The foundation is currently looking for volunteers to begin working.
(B) It is expected to be completed by the end of September.
(C) More space will be available during the winter months.
(D) There is currently no money in the budget for a soup kitchen.

20. (A) be not
(B) has not been
(C) had not been
(D) would not be

Part 7 請閱讀文章，並選出正確答案。

Questions 21-25 refer to the following announcement, survey, and email.

SEEKING: FOCUS GROUP PARTICIPANTS

Max Fame Marketing Firm is looking for participants for an upcoming focus group about a new smartphone that will be released at the end of this year. You will have the chance to use the new model X3 smartphone by Geno-Tech Phones. During the focus group session, you will be asked to discuss your opinion about it in a small group. Afterward, you will be asked to complete a survey about the product. For your time, you will receive a $75.00 gift certificate or a 25%-off coupon you can use to buy the X3.

Date: March 12, 12:00 -1:30 p.m.
Location: The Marimax Complex, Room 112

If interested, please contact Cynthia Jones at (417) 445-4444 or cynthia@maxfame.com.

Thank you for participating in our focus group. Please fill out the following survey and return it to the front desk when you leave.

Name: *Jeremy Lathrom* **Age:** *28*

Contact: *jerlat@jmail.com / (417) 883-3333*

How was your experience with the product today?

	Excellent	Average	Below Average	Poor
Design			✓	
Speed	✓			
Ease of Use		✓		

Would you consider buying the product? ☑ YES / ☐ NO

Please share any comments or suggestions below:

I really enjoyed using the X3. The phone was really fast, and it was pretty easy to learn how to use. However, I think the volume button is in a bad position. It's difficult to press it when holding the phone with one hand. Otherwise, I think this is an excellent product.

What gift would you like to receive? ☑ Gift Certificate / ☐ Coupon

Practice Test

To:	cynthia@maxfame.com
From:	jerlat@jmail.com
Subject:	Focus Group Gift Certificate

Dear Ms. Jones,

When I recently participated in a focus group with Max Fame, I was told that there would be some kind of compensation for it. It has already been more than 6 weeks since I participated in the project, but I have not yet received anything yet. Could you please check on this for me? Let me know if you need any information to verify my participation in the focus group session. Thank you.

Best regards,

Jeremy Lathrom

21. What kind of product is being tested in the focus group?

(A) An online service
(B) A cell phone
(C) A computer
(D) A website

22. What is NOT indicated about the focus group session?

(A) Participants can try using the product.
(B) The participants will talk about the product with each other.
(C) Each participant will help redesign the product.
(D) The participants will receive compensation for their time.

23. What did Mr. Lathrom mention about the phone?

(A) It was too expensive.
(B) The volume button was not easy to use.
(C) It weighs more than he expected.
(D) It felt slow when using it.

24. In the email, the word "compensation" in line 2 is closest in meaning to

(A) reward
(B) deposit
(C) pension
(D) subscription

25. When was the email most likely sent to Ms. Jones?

(A) At the beginning of March
(B) At the end of March
(C) At the beginning of April
(D) At the end of April

Half Test

READING TEST

In the Reading test, you will read a variety of texts and answer several different types of reading comprehension questions. The entire Reading test will last 35 minutes. There are three parts, and directions are given for each part. You are encouraged to answer as many questions as possible within the time allowed.

You must mark your answers on the separate answer sheet. Do not write your answers in your test book.

PART 5

Directions: A word or phrase is missing in each of the sentences below. Four answer choices are given below each sentence. Select the best answer to complete the sentence. Then mark the letter (A), (B), (C), or (D) on your answer sheet.

1. The Manhattan Community Center will be closed for renovations ------- on Wednesday, January 11.

(A) begin
(B) will begin
(C) beginning
(D) has begun

2. The city government encourages employees ------- public transportation when they come to work.

(A) use
(B) using
(C) to use
(D) are using

3. Although the new K510 projector is ------- to other old models, its price is only half as much.

(A) likely
(B) similar
(C) significant
(D) reflected

4. When signing up for a new identification badge, employees need to present ------- of employment to the Personnel Department.

(A) access
(B) basis
(C) proof
(D) label

5. This Monday, all sales clerks may leave one hour before closing ------- their manager asks them to stay in the store.

(A) unless
(B) either
(C) nor
(D) because

6. Doctors and nurses at Bobby Hospital receive overtime pay when ------- work the night shift.

(A) their
(B) they
(C) theirs
(D) them

7. The ------- of a new marketing director at Malcom Electronics will be announced on December 1.

(A) appoint
(B) appoints
(C) appointed
(D) appointment

8. Good leaders try ------- communication among team members whenever possible.

(A) enhance
(B) to enhance
(C) are enhancing
(D) enhanced

9. Hill Hotel employees must contact their supervisors as early as possible ------- they have to be absent from work.

(A) if
(B) soon
(C) though
(D) while

10. Ms. Jackson has been ------- recommended by all of her references.

(A) high
(B) higher
(C) highest
(D) highly

11. To fill a vacant position on the assessment committee, Nico Academy is seeking employees ------- are experienced in the field of education.

(A) which
(B) who
(C) what
(D) how

12. Ms. Lin wants to know when the articles will be ready for ------- to proofread.

(A) hers
(B) she
(C) her
(D) herself

13. ------- being the critics' favorite film at the Zack Film Festival, *Strange Tuesday* did not win an award.

(A) Because
(B) Despite
(C) Nevertheless
(D) For

14. The manufacturer advises that the fine filter ------- at least once every 10 uses of the dryer for best results.

(A) be cleaned
(B) cleans
(C) is cleaned
(D) cleaning

15. The new location of the Wellington Bank is ------- accessible by road or rail.

(A) easily
(B) cordially
(C) promptly
(D) actively

GO ON TO THE NEXT PAGE

PART 6

Directions: Read the texts that follow. A word, phrase, or sentence is missing in parts of each text. Four answer choices for each question are given below the text. Select the best answer to complete the text. Then mark the letter (A), (B), (C), or (D) on your answer sheet.

Questions 16-19 refer to the following notice.

Annual Bonus Leave

The company has decided to institute a new policy -------(16.) employee leave. We will now be rewarding employees for -------(17.) performance. One worker from each department will be chosen based upon the results of the company's employee evaluations. Those individuals will be given an extra three days of paid vacation. --------(18.). Management will select the winners at a meeting on the 21st. The names of those individuals -------(19.) at the company's year-end party on December 28.

16. (A) regarding
(B) in spite of
(C) even
(D) depending on

17. (A) specific
(B) convenient
(C) relevant
(D) outstanding

18. (A) Please sign up for your leave this week.
(B) We are pleased to announce the final list.
(C) It must be taken before the end of the next calendar year.
(D) An incentive system will be introduced.

19. (A) has announced
(B) has been announced
(C) will announce
(D) will be announced

Questions 20-23 refer to the following email.

To: Katherinefm@finefurniture.co.uk
From: Helenjs@finefurniture.co.uk
Re: Excellent performance
Date: June 7

Dear Katherine,

The executives and I were happy to hear that you won the Good Design Award, which is one of the most renowned design awards in the world. We all agree that your contributions to Fine Furniture have been -------(**20.**). Therefore, we are pleased to give you a bonus in the amount of 3,000 dollars. It will -------(**21.**) with your next monthly paycheck on June 25. -------(**22.**), we have decided to raise your salary by 15 percent, effective July 1. -------(**23.**). Your Cozy Chair line has been the bestselling furniture item here for the past few years. We deeply appreciate your hard work and commitment to our company.

Sincerely,
Helen

20. (A) exceptional
(B) reasonable
(C) necessary
(D) affordable

21. (A) pay
(B) paying
(C) be paid
(D) have paid

22. (A) Nonetheless
(B) In addition
(C) In other words
(D) For instance

23. (A) This reflects your excellent performance.
(B) The company will hire more people.
(C) You will be transferred to headquarters.
(D) A pay raise will be given to all the staff members.

GO ON TO THE NEXT PAGE

PART 7

Directions: In this part you will read a selection of texts, such as magazine and newspaper articles, emails, and instant messages. Each text or set of texts is followed by several questions. Select the best answer for each question and mark the letter (A), (B), (C), or (D) on your answer sheet.

Questions 24-25 refer to the following text message chain.

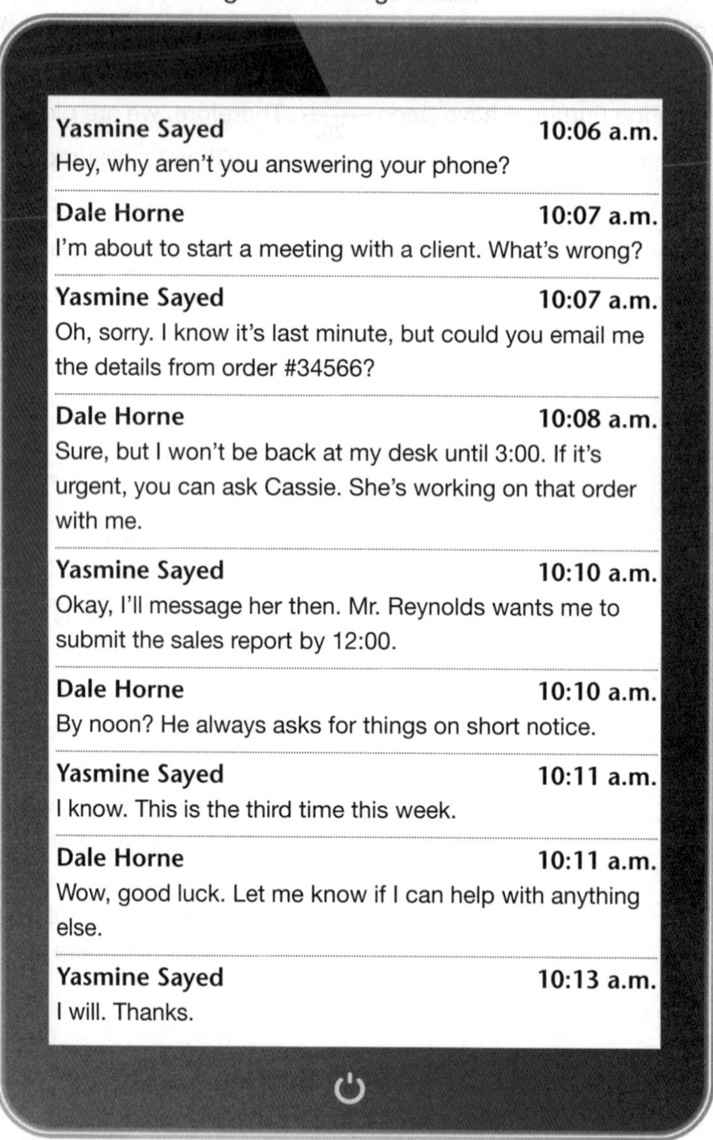

Yasmine Sayed 10:06 a.m.
Hey, why aren't you answering your phone?

Dale Horne 10:07 a.m.
I'm about to start a meeting with a client. What's wrong?

Yasmine Sayed 10:07 a.m.
Oh, sorry. I know it's last minute, but could you email me the details from order #34566?

Dale Horne 10:08 a.m.
Sure, but I won't be back at my desk until 3:00. If it's urgent, you can ask Cassie. She's working on that order with me.

Yasmine Sayed 10:10 a.m.
Okay, I'll message her then. Mr. Reynolds wants me to submit the sales report by 12:00.

Dale Horne 10:10 a.m.
By noon? He always asks for things on short notice.

Yasmine Sayed 10:11 a.m.
I know. This is the third time this week.

Dale Horne 10:11 a.m.
Wow, good luck. Let me know if I can help with anything else.

Yasmine Sayed 10:13 a.m.
I will. Thanks.

24. Why did Ms. Sayed write to Mr. Horne?

(A) To ask about a client's order
(B) To arrange a meeting with a client
(C) To find out more about Mr. Reynolds
(D) To find out when Mr. Horne will be back in the office

25. At 10:10 a.m., what does Ms. Sayed imply when she writes, "I'll message her then"?

(A) She will provide Cassie with the details.
(B) She will contact a client.
(C) She will ask Cassie to send some data.
(D) She will request an extension of time.

Questions 26-28 refer to the following memo.

MEMO

To: All office employees
From: Gail Meyers
Re: New Database
Date: October 15

As you all should know, our new digital database will be introduced this week. Starting on Thursday, all sales reports must be submitted through this new digital system. — [1] —. Just like before, the reports should always include a client ID number, the total sales numbers, and your employee ID number. Hopefully, this new system will make it easier to track our numbers more effectively and produce better results. — [2] —.

Before you can access the new database, you have to apply for a login ID and password from the IT Department. — [3] —. You can do so by submitting a request when you first open the database program. However, it takes 24 hours to process a request, so make sure you apply by Wednesday morning at the latest. If you don't have your ID and password ready by Thursday, you may find yourself behind on work. Just in case, we will accept paper sales reports until the following Monday. — [4] —. Thank you all for your cooperation and effort.

26. What is the purpose of this memo?

(A) To request feedback on a new policy
(B) To announce the quarterly sales reports
(C) To inform the staff of a new department
(D) To alert employees of a change in procedure

27. What are the employees advised to do?

(A) Submit all sales reports by Thursday
(B) Apply for login information by Wednesday
(C) Make paper copies of all their sales reports
(D) Contact the IT Department with any questions

28. In which of the positions marked [1], [2], [3], and [4] does the following sentence best belong?

"However, they will have to be digitized later."

(A) [1]
(B) [2]
(C) [3]
(D) [4]

GO ON TO THE NEXT PAGE

Questions 29-31 refer to the following job advertisement.

Rebound Entertainment is looking for an experienced and driven individual to join our HR team. Our company specializes in localizing mobile games in countries all around the world, with branches in London, Paris, New York, Seoul, Tokyo, and Bangkok. Our HR Department manages employee policies that cross international borders. As part of our team, you'll have the chance to work with people from all around the world and help make connections between them all.

Your duties will focus on supporting our teams on the ground. You will provide advice to managers and supervisors on how to handle issues in the workplace and help with cross-cultural training. You will have to become very familiar with and knowledgeable about our company and its policies. Training will be provided if you are hired. Applicants should have 3-5 years of HR experience, preferably including international experience. Preference will be given to those who can speak additional languages.

We offer a better salary than our competitors, full benefits (including medical and dental), and a relocation bonus if you don't currently live in the New York area. We recommend checking out our website at www.reboundent.com for more detailed information about our company before applying.

29. Where most likely is the job position located?

(A) London
(B) New York
(C) Bangkok
(D) Seoul

30. What is NOT mentioned in the advertisement?

(A) Applicants should have 3 to 5 years of HR experience.
(B) Potential employees will receive training.
(C) The company provides a high salary.
(D) Applicants must speak a foreign language.

31. According to the advertisement, why should applicants visit a website?

(A) To ask questions about a position
(B) To submit an application
(C) To learn more about a company
(D) To schedule an appointment

Questions 32-35 refer to the following online chat discussion.

Ari LeBron [2:00 p.m.]	I'm pleased to share the news that KTD has decided to purchase our accounting software.
Ella Taylor [2:00 p.m.]	Fantastic news.
Ari LeBron [2:01 p.m.]	Indeed. Victor, have you mailed the contract yet? It needs to be sent by 3 p.m. because the post office closes early on Fridays.
Victor Gotak [2:01 p.m.]	No, not yet. I can make it to the post office in 30 minutes. I hope the traffic is not so bad.
Ari LeBron [2:02 p.m.]	Okay. You can charge it to the company account for Grackle, Inc. Accounting. Ella, are you in charge of training the KTD staff members on how to use the software?
Ella Taylor [2:02 p.m.]	Yes, I am. It's already scheduled for Tuesday, May 5.
Ari LeBron [2:02 p.m.]	How many of them are attending the training session?
Ella Taylor [2:03 p.m.]	They said twelve of them are coming.
Ari LeBron [2:04 p.m.]	Really? That's more than I expected. Oh, well. That shouldn't be a problem. We can book the biggest room for the session then.
Ella Taylor [2:05 p.m.]	That's right. Victor, can you book room 304 for the training session? I will need it for 3 hours from 2:00 p.m.
Victor Gotak [2:05 p.m.]	Consider it done.
Ella Taylor [2:06 p.m.]	Thanks.

Send

32. What is the online chat discussion mainly about?

(A) Some new accounting software
(B) An online event
(C) Hiring new staff members
(D) Training new employees

33. What is Ms. Taylor responsible for?

(A) Taking care of the facilities
(B) Writing a contract
(C) Scheduling a business trip
(D) Teaching a training course

34. At 2:05 p.m., what does Mr. Gotak most likely mean when he writes, "Consider it done"?

(A) He will book a meeting room.
(B) He will go to the post office as soon as possible.
(C) He has already modified a contract.
(D) He has already checked the availability of a room.

35. What time does the contract need to be mailed?

(A) By 1:00 p.m.
(B) By 2:00 p.m.
(C) By 3:00 p.m.
(D) By 4:00 p.m.

GO ON TO THE NEXT PAGE

Questions 36-40 refer to the following web page and review.

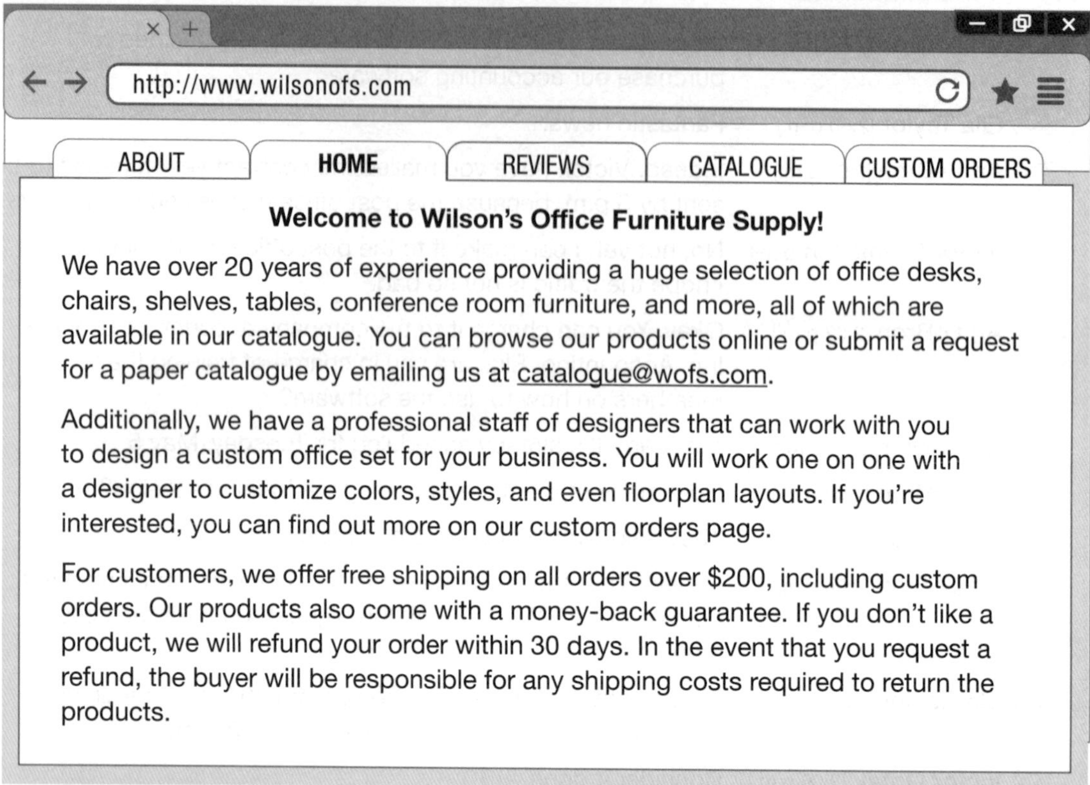

Welcome to Wilson's Office Furniture Supply!

We have over 20 years of experience providing a huge selection of office desks, chairs, shelves, tables, conference room furniture, and more, all of which are available in our catalogue. You can browse our products online or submit a request for a paper catalogue by emailing us at catalogue@wofs.com.

Additionally, we have a professional staff of designers that can work with you to design a custom office set for your business. You will work one on one with a designer to customize colors, styles, and even floorplan layouts. If you're interested, you can find out more on our custom orders page.

For customers, we offer free shipping on all orders over $200, including custom orders. Our products also come with a money-back guarantee. If you don't like a product, we will refund your order within 30 days. In the event that you request a refund, the buyer will be responsible for any shipping costs required to return the products.

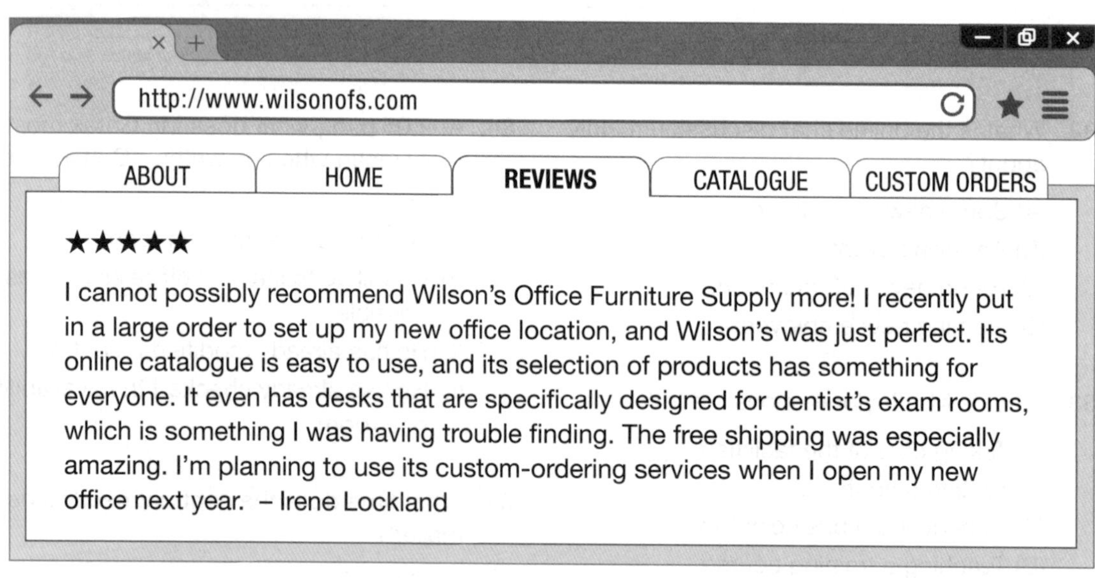

★★★★★

I cannot possibly recommend Wilson's Office Furniture Supply more! I recently put in a large order to set up my new office location, and Wilson's was just perfect. Its online catalogue is easy to use, and its selection of products has something for everyone. It even has desks that are specifically designed for dentist's exam rooms, which is something I was having trouble finding. The free shipping was especially amazing. I'm planning to use its custom-ordering services when I open my new office next year. – Irene Lockland

36. According to the web page, what is true about the refund policy?

(A) No refunds will be issued for completed orders.
(B) Customers have to cover the return shipping.
(C) Products purchased within the last year can be refunded.
(D) Only products worth more than $200 qualify for a refund.

37. According to the web page, why should customers email the company?

(A) To place an order
(B) To ask questions
(C) To check on stock
(D) To order a catalogue

38. What special service is offered on custom orders?

(A) Customers can work with a designer.
(B) Customized furniture can be refundable.
(C) Deposits are not required.
(D) Customers receive a free gift with their order.

39. Where most likely does Ms. Lockland work?

(A) At an IT company
(B) At a print office
(C) At a dental office
(D) At a university

40. What is indicated about Ms. Lockland in her review?

(A) She spent more than $200.
(B) She worked one on one with a designer.
(C) Her business recently closed down.
(D) She made a custom order.

GO ON TO THE NEXT PAGE →

Questions 41-45 refer to the following website, text message, and email.

http://www.fountainfilmfestival.com

The Fountain Film Festival
JAN 14-18

DATE	VENUE	FILM TITLE	DESCRIPTION
JAN 14	Fox Theater	*Moonrise*	A story of an indigenous family that is trying to balance family traditions with a modern world.
JAN 15	Fox Theater	*Pythagoras and Me*	A documentary about an inner-city high school math team that works its way to the national finals.
JAN 16	Willingham Theater	*Deskboys*	An award-winning animated short that follows the life of an architect and his magical pencil.
JAN 17	Olivia Theater	*El Paseo*	A coming-of-age film set in rural Mexico. This film will make you burst into laughter.
JAN 18	West Theater	*The Strange Man*	A rare horror movie that earned an American Best Movie nomination. It has lots of twists and turns.

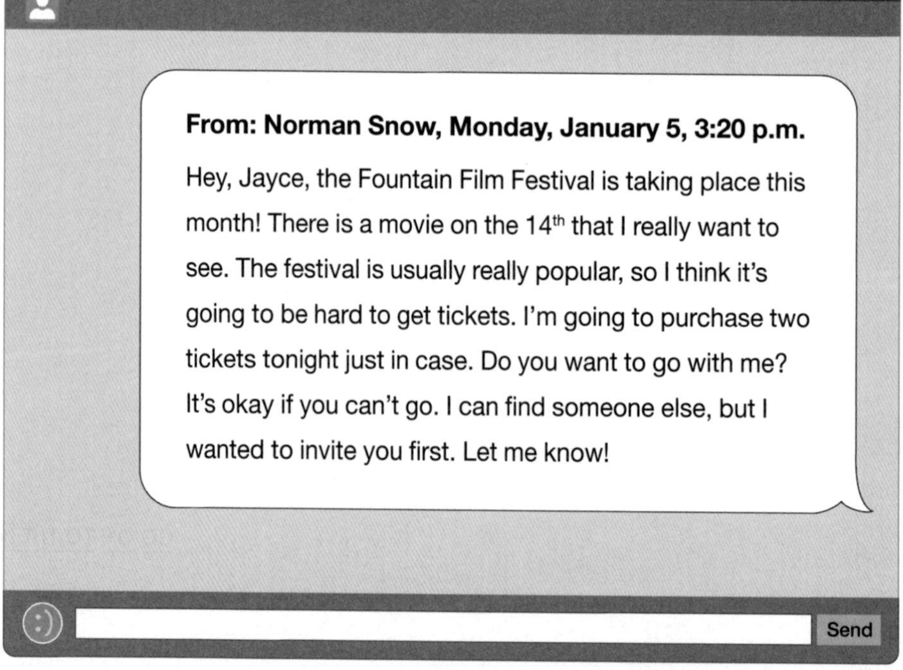

From: Norman Snow, Monday, January 5, 3:20 p.m.

Hey, Jayce, the Fountain Film Festival is taking place this month! There is a movie on the 14th that I really want to see. The festival is usually really popular, so I think it's going to be hard to get tickets. I'm going to purchase two tickets tonight just in case. Do you want to go with me? It's okay if you can't go. I can find someone else, but I wanted to invite you first. Let me know!

To:	n.snow@pontra.com
From:	fountainfilm@fountainfilms.com
Date:	January 10
Subject:	Fountain Film Festival Ticketing

Dear Mr. Snow,

Thank you for purchasing tickets to the January 14 showing of *Moonrise*. Regretfully, I have to inform you that this showing has been rescheduled due to an issue at the Fox Theater. The new date for this film is January 18. It will be shown right after the scheduled film on that day.

If you would like to receive tickets for this showing, please reply to this email, and I will have them sent to you. If you would like to purchase tickets for a different film, I can also help you with that process. In either case, we would like to offer you the tickets at 20% off of the standard price as our way of apologizing for this inconvenience. Thank you for understanding, and we look forward to hearing from you.

Valencia Ortega

Fountain Film Festival Ticketing

41. What genre of the movie is Mr. Snow interested in watching?

(A) Animation
(B) Comedy
(C) Documentary
(D) Drama

42. In the text message, the phrase "taking place" in line 1 is closest in meaning to

(A) selling out
(B) changing
(C) happening
(D) participating

43. What is indicated in the email from Ms. Ortega?

(A) No more tickets are available.
(B) The film festival will host a special guest.
(C) There is a problem with a theater.
(D) A customer's purchase has been confirmed.

44. According to the email, what movie will be showing before *Moonrise*?

(A) *Pythagoras and Me*
(B) *Deskboys*
(C) *El Paseo*
(D) *The Strange Man*

45. What will Mr. Snow receive from the film festival?

(A) A discount
(B) Free tickets
(C) A souvenir
(D) A guidebook

GO ON TO THE NEXT PAGE

Questions 46-50 refer to the following credit card statement and emails.

CREDIT CARD STATEMENT

NAME: Peter Ward
ACCOUNT NUMBER: xxx xxxx xxxx 1123
PERIOD: April 2 – May 1

DATE	VENDOR	AMOUNT
April 6	Meyer's Digital Goods	$65.09
April 7	Giuseppe's Fine Bistro	$88.90
April 13	Benchmark Café	$8.20
April 20	Martin's Apparel	$50.10
April 20	Bags and More	$41.99
May 1	Daniels Office Supplies	$124.95

Email Message

TO: customerservice@martinsapparel.com
FROM: peterward@thenet.com
DATE: May 4
SUBJECT: Problem with credit card charge

Dear Sir or Madam,

I am writing to address an issue with a purchase I made recently on your website. I bought a single pair of jeans that were on sale, but it seems that I was charged twice for them. I didn't notice until I checked my credit card statement and saw that the total charge is exactly twice the price of a single pair of jeans. I'm hoping you can review the order and refund me the value of one pair of jeans.

Sincerely,

Peter Ward

Email Message

To: peterward@thenet.com

From: customerservice@martinsapparel.com

Date: May 6

Subject: Purchase Inquiry

Dear Mr. Ward,

Thank you for your email about the error in the charge made to your order. I personally reviewed your order, and it does seem that you were double-charged due to an error in our purchasing system. I apologize for any inconvenience this may have caused you. I have submitted a refund request, which should be processed within 5-8 business days. The refund will be issued based on your original purchasing method.

Additionally, as a token of our sincerest apology, we would like to send you a coupon worth $30.00 that can be used at any of our store locations. Please provide me with a mailing address so that I can send the coupon to you. We appreciate your business and look forward to serving you again soon.

Best Regards,
Hailey Lombilla
Martin's Apparel Customer Service

46. Where did Mr. Ward make his largest purchase in April?

(A) At a clothing store
(B) At an office supply store
(C) At a restaurant
(D) At an electronics store

47. When did Mr. Ward make the purchase he wants a refund on?

(A) On April 7
(B) On April 13
(C) On April 20
(D) On May 1

48. In the first email, the word "address" in line 1 is closest in meaning to

(A) deal with
(B) advise
(C) consider
(D) request

49. What information does Ms. Lombilla request from Mr. Ward?

(A) How much he spent on a purchase
(B) Where to send a refund of a purchase
(C) Where he would like to receive a coupon
(D) Which form of payment he used

50. How will Mr. Ward most likely receive his refund?

(A) In cash
(B) To his credit card
(C) In the form of a coupon
(D) By check

Stop! This is the end of the test. If you finish before time is called, you may go back to Parts 5, 6, and 7 and check your work.